AN IMMORTAL'S SONG

A DANTE'S CIRCLE ROMANCE

CARRIE ANN RYAN

An Immortal's Song
A Dante's Circle Novel
By: Carrie Ann Ryan
© 2016 Carrie Ann Ryan
ISBN: 978-1-63695-081-5

series reads as if Carrie Ann Ryan peeked at my personal wish list!" – NYT Bestselling Author, Larissa Ione

"Carrie Ann Ryan writes sexy shifters in a world full of passionate happily-ever-afters." – *New York Times* Bestselling Author Vivian Arend

"Carrie Ann's books are sexy with characters you can't help but love from page one. They are heat and heart blended to perfection." *New York Times* Bestselling Author Jayne Rylon

Carrie Ann Ryan's books are wickedly funny and deliciously hot, with plenty of twists to keep you guessing. They'll keep you up all night!" USA Today Bestselling Author Cari Quinn

"Once again, Carrie Ann Ryan knocks the Dante's Circle series out of the park. The queen of hot, sexy, enthralling paranormal romance, Carrie Ann is an author not to miss!" *New York Times* bestselling Author Marie Harte

DEDICATION

To Kennedy.
Thank you for holding my hand.

ACKNOWLEDGMENTS

The Dante's Circle series is about to come to a close and I still can't believe we made it this far. I know I couldn't have done it without so many people.

Thank you Chelle for being my sounding board and for doing my edits. You help make each book better and I adore how your mind works.

Thank you Kennedy for being with me each step of the way and being my motivation.

Thank you to my husband for listening to me gripe and helping me figure out how to live again once my deadlines are over. I love you so freaking much.

Thank you Charity H. for not only doing this cover, but for helping me with so much each and every day.

Thank you to the Sprint Loop for rocking my days!

Meredith, Shayla, Lexi, Carly, Kennedy, Angel, Stacey and anyone that I've missed, thank you!

And thank you readers for joining me on this journey with a human, a merman, and a fae. Because why not, right?

AN IMMORTAL'S SONG

Amara Young has always been on the outside looking in. She's the one lightning-struck woman out of her group who has never felt as if she's belonged. She lost a year of her life caring for her dying friend, but now it's her turn to find out who she is. Only when the time comes, two men stand in her way—two men who claim her as theirs.

Tristan Archer, fae royalty and Conclave member, has waited over nine hundred years for his fate. And now he has two chances. While one knows his path, the other seems blind to what they could have. It will take more than a simple risk for Tristan to finally have what he desires...that is if Amara and Seth can overcome their own uncertainties.

While the other two in his life are fighting themselves and their futures, Seth Oceanus knows exactly what he wants. The younger brother of a Conclave member and relatively young in his realm, he knows he'll have to prove himself so others see him for who he truly is.

As the triad succumbs to their cravings, they will have to fight more than their overwhelming feelings in order to survive.

Warning: Contains an innocent merman, a very talented fae, and a human woman who can outpace them both.

CHAPTER 1

S itting in a bar for hours on end wouldn't help matters, but Tristan Archer figured he might as well try it out. It may take him far longer to get drunk than it would if he were human, yet he figured he'd give it a go. After the hellish few months he'd had, he would try anything at this point.

He ran a hand through his short, auburn hair that tended to look brown in the bar's lighting and sighed. He shouldn't have accepted his friend Levi's invitation to dinner and drinks at Dante's Circle in the human realm. He should have rejected the offer and gone back to the thousand other things he had to do within the fae realm and inside the Conclave.

Tristan wasn't just any fae. He was a nine-hundred-year-old fae prince with responsibilities that lay heavily on his shoulders. He was also a Conclave member, where he helped govern every paranormal realm in existence with another fae member and two others from each race. That was how he'd become friends with Levi, a wizard and prince in his own right.

So here he was, in Dante's Circle, a bar owned and named after a royal blue dragon; the meeting place of seven women and their mates with a history he couldn't immediately comprehend.

Of course, it was because one of those women that he'd rather be in the fae realm instead of the dark bar with oak paneling and photos on the walls that spoke of generations of memories and connections. He'd been here a few times in the past, always on the outside of the circle of lightning-struck woman and their mates, but never fully excluded.

They'd welcomed Tristan into their fold, even if they didn't understand why it hurt him so to be that close to what he couldn't have.

Or maybe they understood all too well. After all, one of their own was the reason for his confusion, his torture. The object of his desire.

"If you keep glowering at her over in the corner, you'll end up scaring her more than she already is," Seth said from his side.

Tristan closed his eyes and took a deep breath, immediately regretting the action as soon as he did. The man next to him smelled of the sea. And hope. His heart ached and his dick filled.

Seth Oceanus was a merman, a friend, and his mate.

His true half.

Or at least one of them.

Not that he or Seth could do anything about it when the other part of their triad didn't feel the same way.

"I'm not glowering," he bit out, his voice a growl.

Seth leaned into his shoulder, and Tristan sucked in a breath, opening his eyes as he looked over at the younger man. While Tristan had seen nine centuries come and go, Seth was only in his mid-thirties. He was a pup compared to Tristan, yet he was still a man, a warrior...and sexy as hell. He was a good two inches taller than Tristan and had spiky brown hair that looked as if he'd rolled out of bed and ran his hands through the strands. He had a decent upper body, but it tapered off to a slender waist and hips. His legs were thick, though not as muscular as Tristan's. Tristan had dreamt of what Seth's tail would look like, but he'd never seen the man in his other form. Though Seth had never seen Tristan in his other form either, as he'd hidden his pointed ears with a cloaking spell. And since he wasn't using his powers, his skin didn't put off the faint glow that usually came with that.

Seth had his hands in his pockets and a frown on his face. Though his eyes wore the wide look of innocence, Tristan knew that was just a bluff. There was nothing inno-

CARRIE ANN RYAN

cent about a warrior of any realm. Seth just hadn't been out of his realm much, and he was taking everything in. That much Tristan knew. If he could get his head out of his ass, Tristan knew he'd be able to help the younger man learn all about the new realms and explore their deep secrets.

Only he wasn't sure he could do that and not lean close, not want to touch or find out every secret the merman held in his own right.

Tristan let out a breath. "Let's head to the table and get this over with."

Seth just shook his head. "That kind of attitude won't help the situation."

"And what will?" Tristan bit out. "Hmm? She doesn't feel what we do. She doesn't have the connection to us that she should. You've seen the way she reacts when we're in the room. She stiffens up and acts as if she can't stand to be with us. She's lightning-struck. Meaning she's not a regular human, and she'll turn into her paranormal counterpart once she mates with her true half. But before that, she should at least *feel* something. All of the other women have in the presence of their mates. Amara does nothing. She doesn't even suck in a breath or lean toward us when we're near. There's no recognition in her eyes."

"There's *something* there," Seth said softly, his voice firm. "If we just ask her…"

Tristan shook his head. "And what will that do? It'll

4

only show us what we already know. She doesn't feel the start of the bond. It'll hurt. She shouldn't be forced to feel that." He couldn't be hurt like that, and frankly, he didn't want to hurt Seth either.

Seth just snorted. "Seriously? You're how old? And yet you don't know that if you just *talk* to a woman, you'll learn infinitely more than glaring from a corner and thinking you know better."

Tristan raised a brow. "I'm not an idiot." Just because he was *acting* like one at the moment didn't make him an idiot. "I know that if we were to actually have a conversation about this, we'd know for sure that she doesn't feel the same as us, but..."

"But you don't want to know for sure," Seth finished for him. "Because once you do, then it's over. We'll end up pining for a mate we never had in the first place. I get it. That's why you and I haven't..." Seth trailed off, and the top of his ears turned red.

Tristan let out a sigh then turned to the man who would be his other mate if things were different. While the two of them could form a bond and find happiness... it wouldn't be the same without their third. Tristan didn't want to hurt the other man by allowing him to think he wasn't enough—even if technically that was true, at least in a sense.

Hence, why all of this sucked ass.

Tristan cupped Seth's face and met the other man's gaze. "I'm sorry," he whispered. "So damn sorry."

Seth gave him a sad grin and shrugged before pulling away. "I still think we should actually speak to her. In fact..." he paused. "I might do that without you. I was staying back because, well...because you're older and more experienced. But I don't want to risk losing something that could be *it* for us because we didn't talk to her. Because we didn't try."

With that, Seth walked away from him and toward the large table in the back corner where the seven lightning-struck women and their mates resided. A few years ago, a few members of the Conclave had the bright idea to mess with the way some humans perceived the paranormal world. Tristan hadn't been part of the decision, nor had Levi or Seth's sister, Calypso.

Humans weren't as "human" as they thought they were. In fact, thousands of years ago, when the residents of the realms mated within each other more frequently, their offspring had begun to have diluted paranormal DNA. Usually, the most dominant supernatural of the couple or triad would be the one to pass on their DNA, and the child would be of that race. However, as time moved on, some couplings had created non-paranormal children. Those children became the human race.

Millennia passed, and the humans forgot where they had truly come from and created their own civilization, separate from the realms. As such, the realms forbade telling the humans of magic or what lay beneath the surface of myth and wards. However, within each human lay a dormant strain or strains of DNA that, in the right circumstances, could be altered enough to force the change.

The Conclave had taken the energy of its past and peoples and created a lightning strike to forever change the lives of seven women. Those women had been friends through the years, though they hadn't known of the supernatural world until it was too late.

Now, one by one, each woman found their mate or mates and, once they finalized the bond, changed into their paranormal self. So far, there was a brownie, a leprechaun, a pixie, and even a djinn. Oh, and he couldn't forget the succubus. Sweet little Nadie didn't appear the type to be a sex-driven paranormal, but since she had mated not only a grizzly bear shifter but also a *dragon*, she seemed to be in good hands.

Of the seven lightning-struck, there were only two left who hadn't changed. Eliana and Amara.

And Amara was *his*.

Only he wasn't sure he and Seth were *hers*.

Tristan shook his head and tried to clear the melancholy. He'd come to the bar because his friend Levi—who had mated the pixie, Faith—had invited him. He would do his damnedest to not mess up their evening.

7

"Hey, you made it," Levi said as he stood from his chair. He gave Tristan a tight hug but had a brow raised. "You okay?" he mouthed. It made sense that the other man wouldn't whisper it, as there were a few shifters in the room and even whispering wouldn't keep the conversation private.

Tristan gave the other man a tight nod before taking the empty seat next to Eliana. The woman smiled at him and pushed over a mug of beer.

"Seth said you were on your way, so Becca got you a beer."

Becca grinned and waved. "I technically don't work here anymore, but Dante doesn't mind if I go behind the bar."

The dragon just raised his pierced brow and took a sip of his drink. "Sure, dear. Whatever you say."

Hunter, Becca's wolf mate, just let out a small growl, his gold eyes full of humor.

Levi marveled at how the group worked together and each had their own stories of war and mating. Yet they all fit together cohesively. He knew most of them had children, as well; though none of them were present at the moment. What he wouldn't do for a taste of what they had.

Without thought, he looked across the table at Amara and froze. She stared at him, a little crease forming between her brows. It was as if she didn't know what to make of him. Yet he knew that wasn't recognition of their fate that he saw within the depths of her chocolate-brown eyes. It was confusion. Wondering why he was there, perhaps? Why he and Seth kept looking at her? Why *she* was there?

He didn't know what she was thinking, what she wanted, but Seth's words rolled around in his brain. It would pain them all when he spoke to her, when he told her what he and Seth were feeling, but standing by and letting *nothing* happen was an even worse mistake.

Tristan knew he wasn't keeping his distance solely because of Amara's feelings. He was scared. So damn scared that he'd lose everything. Things he didn't have in the first place. Because once he spoke to her, once he told her about what he felt and the idea that their fate might be denied, he'd lose any chance at the dreams he had, at the idea of what could be. Things were in limbo at the moment. She didn't know that two men wanted her for their own. Didn't know that their worlds would be forever changed once the truth was out in the open. For now, she was safe, and he and Seth were the only two in pain. Once he revealed all, she'd be in the same agony as they were. He wasn't sure he could do that.

But not doing anything would make him a coward. And Tristan Archer was no coward.

Amara turned away from him then to talk to Lily, the brownie mated to the warrior angel, Shade. But he'd caught the look of worry in Amara's eyes before she moved her gaze from him.

"You will have to find a way to make this work," Ambrose said softly from the other side of him. Ambrose was also a warrior angel. The man was even older than Tristan. In fact, he was pretty sure only Dante was older. He'd seen countless civilizations fall and rise from the ashes, and yet he'd found his true happiness in a demon named Balin, and Jamie, a djinn with eyes only for her men.

Tristan turned to the other man and frowned. "What do you mean?" He looked around them, making sure no one could hear the other man's words. Though that would be out of his hands since practically everyone was supernatural.

"The only ones that can hear me are the ones with senses that allow that," Ambrose continued. "And they know what I'm going to say as it is. We all know what you and Seth are feeling." A shuttered expression passed over Ambrose's face for a moment before he washed it away. "Talk to her. Get her away from here and find out what is going on. Because there is *something* going on."

Tristan shook his head, even as Seth turned toward them. The merman sat on the other side of the table yet still a few people away from Amara. It was as if the group knew the three of them needed to be separated before they took the next step...or at least figured out what that next step was. Only, he was as confused as ever.

"I don't know what you're talking about," Tristan lied.

Ambrose raised a white-blond brow. "Don't I?" The angel shook his head. "Don't let your stubbornness get in the way of what you could have."

Tristan risked a glance at Amara, who had her attention on Lily and Shade rather than the other half of the table. His body pulsated just by looking at her, and he could imagine her dark red hair splayed across his pillow as he claimed her as his own.

Only that wouldn't happen, and he had to get it out of his head.

Ambrose let out a curse under his breath, so low Tristan had almost missed it. "You're more of a lost cause than I was."

Tristan didn't know the story behind the other triad's mating or what exactly Ambrose had meant by that, and frankly, he wasn't sure if he wanted to know. He knew he wasn't thinking rationally when it came to Amara and Seth, and that killed him. He was a Conclave member and a fae prince, damn it. He held power and responsibly and didn't shirk those. Only when it came to his personal life and what was left of it did he seem to be at a loss.

Seth met his gaze at that moment and heat flared between them.

Damn it.

If he and Seth didn't get Amara alone soon and *talk* to her, he'd kick his own ass. His days of staying back from her and being afraid of what might not happen had to be over.

Amara's phone buzzed at that moment, and she looked down at the screen, biting her lip as she did. Tristan wanted to take the phone from her and tell her everything would be okay, that she didn't have to look so worried, but it wasn't his place. And frankly, women in this century didn't appreciate barbarian tendencies. At least, that's what he'd heard from the others.

He was nine hundred years old and hadn't been celibate by far, but he'd also only dated fae as he rarely left the realm other than to go to the Conclave. Fae women had their own set of rules when it came to sex and relationships, so he'd learned to live in that fashion.

Now things were different. The realms were becoming more open to other races as news of the lightning-struck women reached their barriers. He didn't know how to react to a twenty-something human and a thirty-something merman. He was so far out of his depth, he was drowning. Yet he hadn't done anything about the situation, and it had been months since he'd seen Amara at Faith and Levi's home following the wizard attack.

If he weren't careful, his indecision would be his undoing.

Amara stood from her chair then and sighed. "I need

to take this. It's my new boss. Sorry." With that, she grabbed her bag and scurried toward the exit, leaving the rest of the table frowning after her.

Faith let out a curse and shook her head, her dark cap of hair swaying back and forth. "I hate that new job of hers."

Tristan sat up straighter in his chair. "New job?" He'd been in the fae realm for the past month, and hadn't heard that Amara had found new employment. He knew she'd been looking, and had heard that she'd subsequently declined offers of jobs and financial help from her friends.

"She's working as a personal assistant to an asshole downtown," Eliana explained. "Amara applied for the job because the man works in management for a series of hotels, and that's what her degree is in. Yet her job doesn't actually have anything to do with what she's trained for. Instead, she gets him coffee, fetches his dry cleaning, and picks his kids up from soccer practice because, God forbid, he do it himself. And the man's wife is too busy with all her committees and bullshit circles to deal with her own kids, as well."

Tristan fisted his hands on the table. "There has to be a better job out there for her."

"If she'd look for it, I'm sure she'd find it," Lily supplied, a frown on her face. "Because she took a year off, her resume has that gap. It took her a while to find this new job. Now she's afraid what will happen if she quits."

Faith let out another curse, this time louder. "She took a year off to take care of me when I was in that damn coma. She wouldn't let anyone else help because everyone wanted the wards in a neutral place to protect us. And now look what happened." Levi held her close and kissed her temple, whispering something in her ear that Tristan couldn't hear.

Faith had almost died on the battlefield protecting her friends, and Levi had been forced to create a bond between them. The resulting healing period had taken a while—a year for Faith to find her way back to the land of the living. Tristan knew of the events because of Levi, but he hadn't known of Amara's full involvement until now. Her self-sacrifice just made him want her more. Yet he also wanted to find her new boss and teach him a lesson or two when it came to messing with a fae's mate.

"What will it take for her to find something somewhere she's appreciated?" he asked. Seth nodded at him and gave him a small smile. It seemed the two of them were on the same page about Amara. They might not know the exact next steps, but standing back as they were and breaking their fate wasn't working.

"What do you care?" Dante asked. He sat back in his chair, one arm over the back of Nadie's as he absently played with Jace's long, blond hair. The dragon might look relaxed, but there was nothing safe about a dragon, even in sleep.

"She's mine," he stated then looked at Seth, who had a brow raised. "Ours."

"You have a funny way of showing it," Eliana put in. "I mean, it's been how many months since you showed up and joined our group of misfits? Yet all you've done is go all broody over Amara from afar." She nodded at Seth. "And this one's not much better."

"We had our reasons," Seth said, his voice calm. But Tristan heard the undercurrent of anger.

"We've all had our reasons for screwing up our matings, and yet, I don't want Amara hurt," Faith said. "I'm tired," she said softly, and Levi held her closer. "I'm tired of all of us going through hell to find our happiness. I fought the bond because I didn't have a choice when it came to be." She looked at Levi then kissed his chin. "I was an idiot, but I learned to take life as it is and I found that I love this man."

Levi grinned, and Tristan felt a sliver of jealousy slide through him. He didn't want to be jealous. He didn't want to feel like he couldn't have what fate had deemed his. He wanted Amara and Seth in his life. He was far too old to be left wanting.

Yet, he was afraid.

And that wasn't like him.

"Are you going to actually talk to her?" Lily asked. "I

mean, it's good and all that you recognize her as your true half." She looked over at Seth. "That *both* of you have seen that. But you haven't done anything about it. Is it because you're afraid she doesn't feel the same?"

The words were like a slash to the heart. Tristan raised his chin. "And you know that, then? That she doesn't feel that we're her mates?"

Lily shook her head. "We know nothing for sure."

"She won't talk about it with us," Nadie said softly. "But just because she *doesn't* feel it, doesn't mean it's not fate. We're lightning-struck. Since when have we ever done anything normal? Maybe it's because of what kind of paranormal she is. Maybe it's because there's two of you and she's confused." She held up her hand. "Each one of us who found our mate or mates has traveled a different path. Who's to say Amara won't have a completely different journey of her own?"

"You won't know anything until you try," Eliana put in.

"What do you think we should do, then?" Seth asked. "Short of locking her in a room or kidnapping her to one of our realms so we all have to talk it out, I just don't know."

Tristan snorted, a smile tugging at his lips. "I might be old and out of touch, but I can safely say kidnapping is not a way to entice a mate to your side."

"If Malik were to kidnap me, I'd enjoy every minute of

it," Eliana said with a glint in her eye. She'd been dating the lion shifter for a few months, if what Tristan remembered was true. But neither of them had declared their intentions. However, he needed to worry about *his* mating, not someone else's at the moment.

"Dirty," Faith said with a grin and then turned her attention back to Tristan. "Don't kidnap her, per se. But go outside right now and ask her to go with you. She needs to get out of this realm, Tristan." Worry passed over her face. "She hasn't left it in over a year, even though we've all invited her to our other homes."

"She just keeps working for that new boss of hers and burying herself deeper and deeper into her own mind," Becca added and frowned. "I love her, guys. She's our sister. And she's in pain. But we can't be the ones to fix it. You have to be. So take her to the fae or mer realm and figure out what is going on with you three."

"Just know if you put our friend in danger, we'll not only kick you in the nuts, we'll lop them off when we're done with them," Eliana put in and glared.

Tristan did his best to not cross his legs, and Seth pulled in an audible breath. "Are you sure you aren't a dragon underneath?" he asked the only human left at the table.

She just raised her chin. "Who knows? But what I said wasn't a threat, it was a promise."

Tristan nodded. "Hurting Amara is not what I want."

"And what *do* you want?" Dante asked. "Make your decision now before you go after her. Don't break her because you're in doubt."

Seth stood then. "She's ours. I may have let Tristan do the talking just now, but I won't stand back any longer. She's in pain..." He nodded at the table. "Thank you for the push." He met Tristan's gaze. "Coming?"

Tristan stood and looked into the eyes of the man who would be his mate if fate had anything to say about it.

"Yes. Let's get our girl."

Seth grinned, and they turned from the table and made their way to the door Amara had exited the club through earlier. Tristan could feel her; scent her on the other side. They were taking a step that could prove pain-ridden; yet he knew it was the only step he could take.

Without Amara and Seth in his life, he wasn't sure he would be able to continue on. At least not like he had. He'd fought wars, helped build civilizations, loved and lost. But never mated.

Fate had paved the course in front of him, and now he had to take the next step. For himself, for Seth, for Amara, and for what could be.

CHAPTER 2

A mara Young ended her call with her employer and shut her eyes as tightly as she could. She hated the man's voice, his demands, the way he looked right through her as if she didn't exist beyond what she could do for him. Maybe if she wished hard enough, she'd have a new job and wouldn't be forced to work with such an asshole.

Of course, she wasn't a djinn like Jamie, and wishes didn't work that way. Instead, she slid her phone back in her purse and opened her eyes, knowing she'd have to go back into Dante's Circle and face her friends' pitying stares.

And she'd have to face *them*.

Tristan and Seth.

The two men her body wanted, but weren't *hers*. She didn't feel the pull like the other women had described when they'd met their true halves. Tristan and Seth weren't her mates, and lusting after two men without a mating bond wouldn't get her what she wanted. What she needed.

A home.

A family.

A future.

Call her old-fashioned, but she wanted all of that. She'd never had it before. The environment she'd grown up in couldn't really be called a family, and thanks to that and the obstacles life kept throwing in her way, she didn't really have a home or a future like she wanted either.

The door opened behind her and the hairs on the back of her neck stood on end. Seth and Tristan were there. She knew that just as she knew if she didn't move from this spot and walk away, everything would change. She didn't know *how* she knew it, but she did. It wasn't fair that they weren't her mates. Though having two men when she'd never really even had one was selfish in itself. Nadie and Jamie had each been lucky to find their triads, while Faith, Becca, and Lily had found just one man to complete them.

Maybe one day Eliana and Amara would be able to find their fates, as well.

Hers just wouldn't be with Seth or Tristan.

"What's wrong, darling?" Tristan asked as he came forward.

She took a step back without thinking and wanted to kick herself at the look on Tristan's face. It wasn't quite pain—maybe *hurt* in some way? She wasn't sure, but either way, she'd put it there. She hadn't meant to, but as they said…good intentions and all.

"I'm sorry, I just…anyway, what are you two doing out here?" she asked as she gripped the handle of her bag tightly. She didn't feel threatened by the two large men in front of her, far from it, but she didn't feel comfortable either.

She could never feel fully comfortable around them. Not when she wanted to climb their bodies and see just exactly how big and hard they were.

Her cheeks heated, and Tristan raised a brow at her as if he could fully sense her thoughts. She knew he was fae, but didn't know what powers came with that. For all she knew, the man could actually hear her thoughts.

"We came to ask you a question, actually," Seth said as he moved closer to Tristan's side. The two men's arms brushed ever so slightly, and each of them stiffened before relaxing.

Interesting.

If only the three of them were mates. If they were,

then all of this attraction would make sense, wouldn't it? Because there was no way the need she felt was normal. And if she kept telling herself that, maybe she'd start to believe it.

Instead of dwelling on what would never be, she stared into Seth's eyes and became lost. They weren't blue or green, but rather aquamarine, as if the color had been pulled from the shallowest depths of the most glorious ocean. She'd never seen him in his merman form, yet she knew he'd be even more beautiful in it.

Tristan was no slouch either, with those forest green eyes and regal cheekbones of his. She knew he was far older than she and Seth but didn't care. Her life had changed the day the lightning flared within Dante's Circle, and now she knew to take life and the experiences and new revelations that came with it as they came.

"What did you want to ask?" she finally said, her voice husky. She quickly cleared her throat, not wanting Tristan and Seth to know how much she craved them. They were paranormals, looking for mates, someone to spend their lives with in a most momentous fashion. They wouldn't want to waste their time on a human that couldn't be theirs. She wouldn't shift into her other half without her mates, and even then, she might be different.

She'd always been different from the others in some way. Perhaps she was the only one who, despite the lightning, would never shift, would never find a mate in the ways the others had.

Seth studied her face but didn't touch her. Instead, he frowned and tilted his head as if trying to figure out what she was thinking.

He opened his mouth then shut it again before shaking his head as if clearing his thoughts. "We want you to come with us."

Her eyes widened. That was the last thing she'd expected him to say. "Excuse me?" What on Earth had he meant by that, and what did he mean by 'us?'

Were Tristan and Seth together?

Her heart ached at the thought. What if *they* were bonded and she was on the outside looking in. It was a familiar place for her to be, after all.

"Come with us to my realm," Tristan said softly. "We need to speak with you, talk to you about things. And, well, the others said it's been a long time since you've been out of the human realm. Maybe you can call this a vacation of sorts?"

She frowned. "You talked to the others about me? What on Earth do you have to talk to me about that you can't say right here?" She looked around and was relieved to find that there weren't many people walking around them on the sidewalk in front of Dante's Circle. The fact that humans weren't alone in the world wasn't something that was out in the open, and frankly, she didn't want the crazy looks strangers would give her once they over-heard their conversation. She'd had enough of those looks to last a lifetime.

"We weren't talking about you behind your back," Seth put in then cursed under his breath. "What I mean is, they're worried about you, and frankly, so are we."

That put her back up. "Why are you worried? I don't think it's any of your concern."

"Damn it," Tristan muttered. "We're going about this all wrong. Fine, Amara. Seth and I are your mates, yet we know you don't feel the tug of the bond like we do. So we want to go to my realm where we're away from prying ears and eyes and get you away from the job that is putting a strain on you, the one you so clearly hate. We want to figure this all out. The others agree that you should leave here and find some peace, though, frankly, I don't think *peace* is exactly what we have in mind at the moment."

She took a step back at his words, her hands shaking.

"Oh, that was good," Seth said with a snort. "Why don't you just scare her into coming with us? Good plan. Next you'll be listening to Eliana and wanting to throw her over your shoulder and kidnap her."

"If I remember correctly, *you* were the one who mentioned kidnapping first."

Maybe if she turned and ran away right then, they wouldn't even notice her leaving. Amara pinched herself, trying to wake herself up from this bizarre dream. There was *no* way what these two were saying was true.

Kidnapping? Mates?

What. The. Hell.

She needed a drink. Or to wake up. Or *something* that wasn't her standing on the side of the street with her mouth gaping like a freaking fish.

"Whoa," she finally said. She held up both hands, palms facing the two men, and blinked. "I have no idea what the hell you two are talking about, but first, there will be no kidnapping. I know you're stronger and bigger and have magic and crap, but I'm drawing the line at kidnapping."

Tristan's mouth quirked with a smile while Seth winced.

"I didn't mean *actual* kidnapping," Seth said softly.

"Oh, I'm sure you didn't," she lied. She wasn't sure about anything anymore. "Second," she continued, "Why do you think I'm your mate? Because if that's the case, then there's something wrong on my end." Pain slashed at her chest, but she ignored it. "I'm a bad bet, so you'd better just walk away."

"Amara," Tristan whispered. "You're anything but a bad bet."

"That's why we want to take you away from here and figure out what's going on," Seth added.

She shook her head and pressed her lips together. The

back of her eyes burned, and she did her best not to cry. Crying was for weaker mortals, and frankly, she'd cried enough in her life.

Something the men had said earlier finally penetrated all the other monumental things filling her brain.

"Wait. The others said I should go? As in they don't want me here anymore?" Anger slid over her like a warm blanket, and she let her hands fall to her sides, curling them into fists.

Seth shook his head quickly. "That's not what they were saying, Amara."

"They only want you to breathe," Tristan added. He stepped toward her, and this time, she didn't pull back. When he put his hand on her cheek, she gasped at the shock of his skin against hers. "Come with us, Amara. Let's figure everything out together. It's long past time we actually talk."

"I...what if you're wrong," she whispered, voicing her deepest fear.

"I'm never wrong," Tristan said smoothly.

Seth let out a cough. "I'm wrong sometimes about other things, but not about this." She looked over as he rubbed his fist over his heart. "I *know* what I feel. And I'm not going to back away because things are different than how they normally are."

She didn't know what to say, what to think. It was all too much. But...what if what they were saying was true?

What if she *was* their mate and there was an actual future for the three of them?

She'd never backed down from anything in her life, even when it had almost killed her. Maybe she should take the risk, knowing full well that if the two men in front of her were wrong, she'd break worse than she ever had before.

The others wanted her gone, and even if it wasn't rational in her mind, she didn't want to go back in there and see their faces. She didn't want to see the looks of pity and hope she couldn't quite understand. The others had their mates, and Eliana...well, Eliana might understand, but she had Malik.

Amara had no one.

Yet she *might* have a glint of a chance with the two men in front of her.

Seth reached around and touched her hip while putting his other hand on Tristan's back. The three of them formed a unit, touch to touch, and she gasped at the contact.

"Okay," she whispered, knowing she might be making the biggest mistake of her life. "Take me to your...realm."

Tristan smiled full-out while Seth let out a relieved breath. "Then let's get out of here. Do you want to say goodbye to the others first?"

She blinked. "You mean we're going right now?" She needed to pack. Or brush her hair. Or something.

Tristan lowered his arm while Seth moved back. She immediately felt the loss. She was already a goner.

"Why not right now?" Seth asked. "It's Friday, and you don't work weekends." He paused. "At least, you shouldn't. Right?"

She worked seven days a week and was on call twenty-four hours a day, but she wasn't sure she wanted to say that.

Tristan narrowed his eyes. "You need another job, Amara. That's just one thing we'll discuss this weekend."

She raised a brow. "I'm not going with you if you're going to spend the entire time telling me what to do. I lived with someone who did that most of my childhood, and I'm not going back to that kind of life." She closed her mouth quickly as soon as she'd revealed that tidbit. The other women knew of her past, but no one else did, and she'd be damned if she'd let these two find out. They didn't need to know how she'd grown up. She was past that.

She was healed.

Again, if she kept telling herself that, then one day, she'd believe it.

"We'll discuss that, as well," Tristan said smoothly.

Seth let out an aggravated breath. "What he means is, we'll talk about all sorts of things. We're not going to tell you how to live your life. I promise." He turned to Tristan, who raised a brow before looking at her again. *"We promise."*

She let out a breath. "Okay, then. Let's...go, I guess?" That hadn't come across very confident. This was a life-altering decision. Amara could do better than that. "I don't need to say goodbye to the girls. Apparently, they're ready for me to be gone." She couldn't help the bite in her tone, and by the looks on their faces, the men seemed to notice. "To the fae realm?"

They both nodded, and Tristan held out a hand to each of them. "Let's be off, then."

She gripped his palm and let out a slow breath. "Okay. One question, though. Why are we going to the fae realm and not the mer one?" She looked at Seth, who shrugged.

"He's older." She snorted, and Seth grinned at her. "Plus, the fae realm isn't underwater so it's a little easier for you to acclimate." Her eyes widened, and he reached out to grip her other hand. "Don't worry. When we go to my realm, I'll help you. You won't drown. I promise."

She knew Faith and Levi had been to that realm before and *had* almost drowned, but that was another's doing, not the merpeople's.

Tristan squeezed her hand and met her gaze, and she knew that with this one step, everything would change. She wouldn't just be Amara, lonely human with no future anymore. She'd be...well, she didn't know what she'd be, but she'd change. Because there was no way she'd come out of whatever happened next the same.

Tristan looked up into the sky and muttered a few words under this breath, and Amara gasped. Purple and blue lights surrounded them, swirling into a vortex that didn't look like Levi's or any other's that she'd seen. Instead, the colored tendrils wrapped around her, Tristan, and Seth, their warmth and energy pulsating along her skin until she couldn't see the bar or the street anymore.

Before she could figure out what that meant, or even say something about what was going on, the colors faded away and she no longer stood in front of Dante's Circle in the city she'd grown up in.

Instead, she was in a new realm, a new place she'd never seen before.

Tristan let go of her hand but stood close, as did Seth. She looked at them a moment before letting her attention fall to the beauty surrounding her. Green. So much green. Though they'd landed in a clearing, tall trees reached toward the sky, the girth of their trunks and limbs speaking of centuries of life and history. Flowers and green vegetation covered the ground, and a dirt path cut through the meadow as if people had traveled amongst this beauty for years yet didn't want to harm it other than this one path.

The sky was a dark blue, slightly different than the

one she'd grown up under. The magic in the air sizzled but didn't harm. It was as if it had always been welcome. As if the world had matured and evolved under the heavy weight of the fae's power.

In the distance, she could see a large mound with a shaded doorway at the edge. She'd grown up reading fantasy and lore and had heard of the fae, but as with all myths, she knew that it wasn't all truth. Not with as many supernatural races as she'd met in the past few years.

"Wow," she breathed, and Seth chuckled.

"I know, right?" he said as he came to her side. "I've only been here once, and that was with my sister, Calypso for a Conclave thing. I've never really ventured out and explored."

"Well this is your lucky day, then," Tristan said, pride and a little bit of anxiety in his voice. "I took us near my home instead of directly inside like I usually do because I wanted you to see this." His gaze was on the mound and not her, but Amara knew he still had his attention on her. Despite the fact that she didn't feel the tug she should, *he* apparently did, and he wanted her to like his home.

Unsure of what to say or do, she placed her hand in his. "It's beautiful. Thank you for showing me your realm."

He squeezed her hand while Seth took her other one again. "Thank you." Tristan cleared his throat. "My home is behind wards right through there." He gestured with his free hand down the path toward a grouping of trees. "The mound is where our Court is and most of our business happens."

"Court?" she asked as they made their way down the path. "Like Seelie and Unseelie?"

Tristan winced and looked over his shoulder. She winced, as well, aware she'd said something she shouldn't have. "We don't have those Courts anymore," he said finally. "I'll explain it all once we're at my home."

She nodded and kept her mouth shut. There was apparently a lot of history she didn't know, and she didn't want to end up saying the wrong thing.

Tristan held out his free hand in front of him once more, and the image in front of her shimmered before peeling away. Instead of trees, a large stone home—or castle, rather—stood in front of them, tall, proud, and intimidating as hell.

"This is home," he said simply.

But there wasn't anything simple about the stone structure in front of her. It spoke of countless histories and paths she'd never thought to take. The man at her side was over nine hundred years old according to Faith. Amara couldn't even comprehend what that truly meant in terms of experiences and memories.

For all she knew, this old building in front of her was

his *new* one and he had even older ones dotted along the landscape.

She wouldn't hyperventilate, but damn, she was close.

Amara rolled her shoulders back, knowing she needed to be strong with what was to come. These two men thought she was their mate, and even though she desperately wanted that to be the case, she couldn't allow herself to hope. Because if they were wrong and it was merely sexual attraction, then she could lose everything; both the things she had and the things she hoped to have.

If she faced what was to come head-on, she'd be able to look in the mirror with some semblance of respect. Her heart ached with the fact that she didn't feel the tug, the pull she should. She'd always been different, and this just cemented that.

Amara was just so tired. She'd spent years running from her past, only to end up in job after job that sucked the life out of her. She had nothing to show for her hard work except circles under her eyes and pity from others.

Lost didn't begin to cover how she felt. She wasn't like the other lightning-struck. She'd never been. She never took chances because she had to fight for what little she had and she didn't want to lose that, too.

Yet now, look at her.

In a new realm, between two men who wanted her as their own.

Could she do this? Could she give in?

She sucked in a breath as they walked through the large doorway, the men on either side of her watching her reactions. Maybe she could roll with the punches. Maybe she could...take that chance.

Maybe this would be the adventure she never thought to have.

It was past time, after all.

MALIK

Malik awoke with a shout, his body sweat-slick and his pulse racing. The nightmare had come again, this time with a vengeance. The Pride had burned around him, their echoing screams never leaving his memory. He was a lion shifter, a prince, and would one day be the Leo of his people.

And yet, he had no successor.

No mate. No bond.

If he didn't make changes soon, he knew his dreams would become prophecy, instead of simply nightmares.

With a sigh, Malik got out of bed and strode naked to his dresser where his phone chirped. The sound had thankfully pulled him from the dream where he'd stood alone amongst the death and destruction of his people.

Glancing at his cell, he saw that Tristan, his long-time friend, had texted him, letting him know he wouldn't be available for the next few weeks. It seemed his buddy had taken the leap and was doing his best to find a bond with not one, but two mates.

He was happy for Tristan, so damn happy, but he knew *he* wouldn't have that. He'd been alone for too long. He might not be as old as Tristan or some of the other races, but lion shifters were different.

With that nightmare and now Tristan's news, Malik knew he had to do what was expected of him. He didn't want to, but it was past time he did what he had to in order to protect his people.

A knock on the door pulled him from his thoughts, and he quickly pulled on his jeans. He'd been sleeping in the middle of the damn day since he hadn't had a chance to sleep before that. But now, the person he needed to see was here.

When he opened the door, he did his best not to lean forward and inhale Eliana's sweet scent. His lion loved that scent and wanted more of it. They both wanted to roll around in it and let it seep into their skin. And because of that, he knew it was time to do what he had to do.

"Come in." His tone was short, and Eliana raised a brow at it. It hadn't escaped her attention that he hadn't leaned down to kiss her or rub his nose along her cheek like he was prone to.

"Were you sleeping?" she asked. "I thought you said I should meet you here for dinner, but if you need to go back to bed because of work, I don't mind." From the heated look in her eyes, he knew what she wanted to do in bed.

"I'm sorry you came over here, Eliana. I should have called you."

She tilted her head. "What's wrong, Malik?"

"It's over." There. He'd said it. As long as he did this quick, it would be okay. Just like tearing off a bandage. "It was fun while it lasted, but I'm looking for something long term and you're not it."

He was a fucking asshole, but if he didn't push her away, he'd do something monumentally stupid. Like mate with a human. His kind *couldn't* mate with humans. Not that she knew about his kind and what went bump in the night. Her friends might, but Eliana didn't. And he knew the secrets of his kind were far more important than a human's feelings. Even if it killed him to break her heart…and perhaps his.

Lions couldn't mate with humans because of the way their bonds were created. They *chose* to mate, rather than allowing fate to decide. And because he hadn't been able to find someone to mate with in all this time, he'd have to allow the Pride to choose his female. If Eliana were anything other than human, he and his lion would have chosen her. But because his fate was fucked up, he'd never have her.

And he had to push her away before the other lions heard of her existence...or before he fell even more in love with her.

Tears filled Eliana's eyes and her hand shot out. He let the slap come, relishing the ache.

"You bastard. You're looking for forever but I'm just a good fuck? Is that it?" Her chest heaved and she took a staggered step back. "I thought...I thought..." She shook her head. "It doesn't matter what I thought because, apparently, I was wrong. I'm an idiot. Well, fuck you, Malik. Go find your perfect wife or whatever the fuck you're looking for. I don't need this. I'm better than that." She turned on her heel and opened the door, practically running from him.

She hadn't slammed the door on her way out; instead, she'd left it partially cracked, as if she couldn't wait to get away from him.

He didn't blame her. He'd been callous, but it was for the best.

Malik slowly closed the door and went back to his phone so he could text Tristan. The man was going to mate with a human and he couldn't understand that, but he'd give his friend his best. Then he'd do his duty to his people and mate with a lioness.

He'd lost the one woman who could have been his. If only she weren't human...

CHAPTER 3

S eth Oceanus pressed his lips together and tried not to smile too broadly or throw up from nerves. Neither would show the others that he was ready for what was to come, but he wasn't sure he could help it. He was just so damned excited about what was happening, even if it scared the hell out of him.

He wasn't as old as Tristan, and had seen far more war and pain than Amara had, but from the haunted look in her eyes when she thought he wasn't looking, he knew she'd seen more than he would ever want for her. He'd spent his life so far building his strength so he could protect not only his people but also what would one day be his. He wasn't a prince in truth or anything, not like Tristan, but his family held power. His sister was one of the two Conclave members for the mer realm, and he was in charge of her safety. Though he knew she could protect herself far better than he could on any given day. She *was* older than him with more experience, after all.

He'd jumped in headfirst with all of that training, however, knowing he would one day need it for his mate, as well. Or mates as it turned out. He couldn't believe his luck and fate.

Only he *could*, considering the fact that Tristan refused to truly speak with him and Amara didn't feel the potential of a bond between them. If it weren't for bad luck, he wouldn't have any luck at all.

Hell, that hurt. It felt like someone had stuck a hot poker in his heart and twisted. The thought of having a one-sided bond made him want to retch or throw something across the room. But he did neither. Instead, he tried to focus on what was at hand and find a way to make it work for everyone. He couldn't give up, even if the odds against them seemed insurmountable.

Amara hadn't spoken a word since she'd asked Tristan about the Seelie and Unseelie out in the clearing, and he couldn't blame her. He didn't know all the history in the fae world, and Tristan had seemed almost worried at her question, as if he hadn't wanted others to overhear.

It was clear that both he and Amara had a lot to learn about Tristan's people. Because of his age, the other man probably had a leg up when it came to the histories of many of the realms, but Seth wouldn't just lie back and allow his future to pass him by without a fight. He'd figure it all out. He always did.

He'd also noticed that as they moved closer to Tristan's home, Amara had seemed to steel her spine. She'd rolled her shoulders back and taken a deep breath once they breached the front door. He could only hope that her actions meant they would be able to peel back the layers of what could be between them and find a way to make a bond out of hope and a promise.

"So," Tristan said with an odd grin. "This is my home."

Seth looked at Amara, who blinked at him. "It's...big," Seth said slowly.

Amara laughed quietly and bumped her shoulder against his arm. "It is that."

He grinned down at her, liking the way they shared this experience together. Her eyes glittered up at him, and he wanted to lean forward and tuck her hair behind her ear. He only barely resisted the urge.

Too soon, he told himself.

For now.

Tristan snorted and shook his head. "I'd make a joke along the lines of, 'well if you think this is big,' but I think we should probably talk a bit more first."

Seth threw his head back and laughed, and Amara joined him, the tension in the room lessening dramatically. Nothing like a dick joke to bring people together.

Tristan just smiled at him and shook his head. "Before

we talk about the giant elephant in the room that concerns the three of us, perhaps we should take a seat in the sitting room. I'll tell you about the fae world. I know it might have seemed like I was angry or worried when you asked about the Seelie and Unseelie earlier, Amara, and while I wasn't truly either, there *is* a history there that not everyone is...peaceable about." He held out his hand to Amara. "Come, and I'll tell you a story."

She slid her hand into Tristan's, and Seth took her other hand as they made their way to the other room. He'd have taken Tristan's hand, as well, but he wanted to touch Amara as often as possible. He knew, like himself, Tristan was bisexual and felt the same pull he did. When it was time, the two of them would form a connection of their own, but first they would concentrate on Amara. They would have plenty of time for everything else later.

At least, he hoped.

They took a seat on one of Tristan's large couches, the leather a startling cream against the darkness of the walls and floor. The entire place was a little intimidating, and Seth figured it would take time to get used to.

"The Seelie and Unseelie as you've most likely read about in fables and myths is actually quite true," Tristan began. "Or rather, it *was* true. A thousand years ago, about a century before my birth, there was a great war between the two Courts. The two queens finally let their relative distrust and hate of each other come to fruition,

44

and my realm almost faded to extinction." He frowned. "Faded isn't the correct word. There was nothing soft and into the mist about the way my people died at the hands of the other Court because of where their magic came from. We aren't like wizards and witches where the dark and light magic necessarily means death and life. The two Courts simply had a different place where we pulled our magic and ability to...live from. One wasn't wrong, one wasn't right. And yet, it took a war where our people almost killed each other entirely to understand that."

Amara reached out and gripped Tristan's hand. Seth wasn't close enough, but he gave the other man a nod. The merpeople had their own dark histories, and there were still battles to be fought within his borders. No realm could ever truly be at peace, not with free will and choice, but at least they weren't at war. And from the look of the fae realm now, neither were Tristan's people. But, apparently, it had taken great sacrifice to come to this point.

"Once the dust settled and people began to rebuild, our lives changed irrevocably and the Grey Court formed. No longer were we two Courts that lived and died by the code of light and dark. Instead, we were *one*. We're a Court of light *and* dark...as well as grey. Not pure, not evil, but...alive. My family became high leaders; my father, the king."

Amara sucked in an audible breath and Seth squeezed

her shoulder. He'd known of Tristan's lineage, but he wasn't sure she had.

"I was the first son born under the Grey Court and, therefore, a Grey Prince. I have older siblings, as well as younger ones, but I was the first." He snorted. "People like to say that often and use it in their own histories when it comes to how the Grey Court came to be." He paused before shaking his head. "Anyway, there are some who want to go back to the world of light and dark, of Seelie and Unseelie, but I'm not sure that could ever happen. It's been centuries, and our people are finally able to live without the fear of death when it comes to the other side of magic." He lifted Amara's hand to his mouth. He brushed a kiss on her knuckles that sent shivers down her body. Seth could practically feel that kiss and he wanted one of his own. "That's why I was… quiet when you asked your question outside the wards. It might have looked like we were alone, but others could have been near enough to be hidden within their own wards." He gestured around the room with his free hand. "There are many, *many* fae within our realms, though most would rather hide in the shadows until they are ready to be seen. There are countless people within these walls, though they're all working so they haven't introduced themselves." He grinned. "I think they're keeping themselves scarce since it's the first time you're here."

Seth nodded. He'd heard the others walking about as

they cleaned, cooked, and talked amongst themselves. He was sure that Amara hadn't though, and he was glad Tristan had mentioned it. He wasn't sure where Tristan's family lived or if they were close, but he'd find out one day. That was why they were here, after all.

Amara stood up then, a frown on her face. "Thank you for telling me all of that. I'll try to be careful next time. I don't want to start an issue or something over a history I don't know. As for people being here?" She just smiled and shook her head. "Your life—both of your lives —is so different than mine. I come from..." her voice trailed off. "Well, let's just say I don't come from anything quite like this. In fact, I don't know if I can fully comprehend your worlds. I'm just me. A human." She met both of their gazes. "A human who doesn't feel the bond like you two do." Tears filled her eyes and she blinked them away. "I don't want to hurt either of you, but what if you're wrong? What if the bond doesn't truly exist and you're just attracted to me...and each other? We'll all end up hurt if we pursue this and nothing comes of it, don't you understand that? I don't want you two hurt because of me."

Seth quickly stood and cupped her face. Her skin was so soft underneath his palm. Soft, pure, and *his*. "This isn't your fault. We're all out of our depths here, but no matter what happens, it is *not* your fault. Please say you understand that."

47

She didn't say anything, but a tear finally fell down her cheek. He brushed it away with his thumb. Amara should never cry. He'd tear apart anyone who dared to make her feel as though she should.

"At least try, sweetling. Please." At her slight nod, he did what came natural and lowered his head. She gasped into his mouth, and he pressed his lips to hers. The electric shock between them only pushed him to kiss her deeper.

Her hands hesitantly went to his side, her fingers slowly trailing over the top of his shirt. He wanted to strip it off so she could touch skin, so he could feel her fingers along his sides, his stomach, his chest...but he knew that would be moving too fast.

When she slid her tongue along his, he let out a small growl and had to pull back, his chest working hard as he tried to take in breaths. Her eyes were wide, her pupils dilated, and her mouth parted, her lips swollen from his kisses.

"I think I can try if you're going to keep kissing me like that," she finally said, and he grinned.

"Damn," Tristan said from the side.

Seth looked over at the man who would be his mate and had to suck in a breath. The man was stunning. He'd let his glamour fall, and his skin glowed ever so slightly while his ears became pointed. And from the look in his eyes, he wanted them both. Badly. Seth looked at Amara to make sure she was okay, and she merely smiled at Tristan, her eyes wide but not full of fear.

Tristan licked his lips. "That was…that was even better than I thought it would be." He took a step closer. "Do you think I could have a taste?"

"From which one of us?" Amara asked as she lowered her eyelids.

"Both, darling," Tristan said as he brought her into his arms. "Both." He crushed his mouth to hers and Seth let out a moan of his own.

Holy. Hell. Seth wanted this to work. *Needed* this to work. Yes, he was worried that it might not happen, that the bond wouldn't be there because of the way Amara had come into their lives, but he couldn't think about that. She would be theirs, and they would find a way to make everything as fate intended. And because they weren't in danger like the other lightning-struck had been when they'd followed their paths to mating, he, Tristan, and Amara could take it slow.

Only he didn't *want* to take it slow.

He wanted to strip them both and make love to them until the bond snapped into place and he could have his fill.

He may be a virgin, but he hadn't been completely chaste. He'd just spent his time working to protect his people, knowing there would be time eventually where he could focus on his body and needs. Only now, the only two people he ever wanted to share this experience with were in front of him, their lips on one another as Tristan took what was *theirs*.

Seth couldn't wait to find out exactly what he'd been missing all of these years. Sure he was slightly nervous, but with Tristan and Amara, he knew there would be nothing wrong with what they did. He had to believe in fate, had to believe in a future that included them all. There wasn't another option.

When Tristan pulled back, and Amara swayed on her feet, Seth moved to catch her. His arms wrapped around her waist and his fingers brushed along Tristan's forearm. Seth sucked in a breath, need coursing through him.

"Now you two," Amara whispered. "Show me. Show me what could be."

"Well, we can't deny the lady," Tristan said with a grin then cupped the back of Seth's head. Tristan pressed his lips to his and Seth moaned once more. He still had Amara in his arms, her taste on his tongue, but he had Tristan in front of him, setting the tone. Their tongues clashed together, their kiss far more violent with need than either of the two kisses before. Seth had been kissed by both men and women before, but nothing like this.

There was only one Tristan Archer, and from the way the fae kissed and nibbled, the man knew it.

When Tristan pulled back, Seth had to keep sucking in breaths to keep his head from going dizzy. Amara breathed at his side, and he knew that she was turned on by what she'd just seen.

Seth Oceanus was one lucky soul.

"You two need to do that again," Amara said with a laugh. "Often. And as many ways as possible." She fanned her face with her hand and winked. "I'd ask what's next, but I'm a little worried we'll all end up naked in a sweaty pile without talking first."

Images of her pale white skin against the darker shade of Tristan's and the tan of his own filled his mind. He wanted that. Desperately.

He must have made some sort of noise, because both Tristan and Amara stared at him, want and desire evident in their gazes.

Tristan was the first to speak after clearing his throat. "I agree...we should talk first. But what of? We need to get to know each other, need to find out exactly who we are, separately and together."

"But we won't know if we're truly mates until we try," Amara added, her voice soft. "And the only way to do that..."

"Is to make love," Seth finished for them all. "Are you ready for that?" he asked them both.

She met his gaze then looked at Tristan with equal intensity. "I *want* us to be mates. And I can't believe I'm saying this when we're just getting to know one another in truth, but I want you both. In bed and out. And if getting into bed and having your hands on me and each other is a way to find out if we're all mates, then I want to take that step. I don't want it to break us, and it's scary as hell to think it could if the bond doesn't happen. Doing this so soon might be crazy in another context, but we aren't other people. We're us. And I want to take that step."

"*Are* you ready?" Tristan asked, his voice serious.

Seth held his breath, waiting for her answer.

"We'll never be ready for either outcome, but I know I'm ready to try," Amara answered. "Is that good enough? Are you willing to risk it? Risk what might never happen?"

"I've been ready since I first saw you in Faith's home," Seth said quickly. "I've wanted to know you, wanted to know what makes you smile, what makes you sad. I want to know everything, and no matter what, I plan to find out. But you're right, with the sense of unknowing surrounding us; it only hampers what could be. So, yes, I'm ready to make love to you." He chuckled deeply. "Beyond ready, actually."

"And with that, I say we go upstairs where I have a very large bed. We can continue this conversation there." Tristan lowered his voice. "In detail."

Seth licked his lips and held back another moan. He wanted Tristan to lower his voice like that again, this time when the other man was either inside Amara or himself. He followed them both through the long hallway and up the giant staircase. One day soon he'd ask for a tour, but first, he wanted to know them both. In every way. If they didn't take this step and find out if the bond would form with the three of them making love, then he knew they'd never be able to move on.

When he'd left his home that morning, he'd never have thought this would be where he'd end up, but he wouldn't—couldn't—let it slip through his fingers. Instead, he'd take it as it came and learn everything he could about Amara and Tristan along the way.

They reached the bedroom, and he could practically feel the nerves radiating from Amara's skin. She had her lips pressed together so tightly, he was afraid she'd cut them with her teeth. It seemed the walk from the sitting room to Tristan's large bedroom had put doubt in her mind.

"We can wait," Seth said softly, though he hadn't wanted to say it at all. "If you're not ready, we can just talk."

Amara shook her head then took a deep breath. "I'm fine, really. It's just seeing that monster of a bed in the center of the room like that with the draperies and things; it kind of made it all real, you know?"

Seth grinned despite himself. "It *is* a pretty big bed."

"Enough room for the three of us," Tristan added. He came closer to them both, slowly undoing the buttons on his shirt. Seth licked his lips at the tantalizing flashes of skin revealed as Tristan's nimble fingers worked. "I want to taste you, Amara."

She tipped her chin up, and Tristan lowered his head, kissing her softly. While they slowly moved toward one another, their hands roaming along each other's torsos, Seth stripped off his shirt, wanting skin-to-skin contact as soon as possible. He moved toward the two, coming up to Amara's back. She gasped into Tristan's mouth as Seth slid his hands over her hips, brushing his fingers along Tristan's.

Tristan pulled back and took her chin in his fingers before turning her head slightly. "Kiss him, darling. Let him taste you, as well."

Seth lowered his mouth as soon as Tristan had begun to speak, desperately hungry for her. Her tongue tangled with his as she relaxed, her back relaxing against his front. His cock rested against her ass, and he slowly tilted his hips back and forth, the friction almost his undoing.

Amara tasted of sweetness and Tristan. He couldn't wait to see how she tasted *everywhere*.

When he pulled away, Tristan tugged on her hair and took her mouth again. It seemed Tristan wanted to be the one to direct them. While Seth would normally be okay with that, he also wanted to make sure Tristan got his pleasure, as well. The three of them would have to ensure they *always* looked out for the other two in desire, need, and communication.

"Can we taste you, as well?" Seth asked Tristan, his voice husky. Tristan raised a brow as Amara's hands slid to his belt buckle.

"I like Seth's idea," she purred. "First one to make him pop wins?" she said over her shoulder, and Seth grinned.

"Don't dare me, sweetling." With that, he dropped to his knees in front of Tristan, and Amara joined him.

Tristan let out a groan. "I thought we'd make Amara come first." He might have said the words, but he didn't push them away when they pulled his pants down and had his dick in their joined hands.

Seth pumped Tristan once, loving the way Tristan groaned again. The other man was thicker than Seth but not quite as long. He couldn't wait to feel this inside him and watch the way Amara writhed while filled with both.

"You can make me come, too," Amara said as she ran her small hand over Tristan's length. "You can make me come multiple times in fact. But first, I want you in my mouth."

Seth couldn't help but agree and watched as Amara took Tristan's cock into her mouth, her lips wide. She bobbed her head, humming slightly. The other man groaned loudly once more and tangled one hand in her hair while finally removing his shirt with the other.

"Seth," Tristan bit out, the muscles in his neck strained. "Our girl is wearing far too many clothes."

"I totally agree." With that, Seth pulled Amara back and stripped off her shirt and bra quickly. So quickly that she just blinked at him.

"Impressive," she said with a grin.

"No, Amara, *you're* the impressive one," Seth breathed. "Fuck, your nipples are pink and perfect. I can't wait to get them in my mouth and see what happens when I suck on them for hours. Will they turn red like cherries? Will you come by my tongue on your breasts alone?"

Amara rubbed her thighs together and moaned.

"Fuck this," Tristan said and pulled away before he stripped off his shoes and pants. "I need to taste you, Amara. All of you. You can suck my dick later." He said the latter to both of them before pressing a hard kiss to Seth's lips. "Take off your pants."

Seth wasn't sure if the fae was talking to him or Amara, but he stripped completely anyway. His dick ached something fierce and bounced on his stomach, leaving a trail of wetness in its wake.

Before Seth could blink, Tristan had a gorgeous, naked Amara on her back on the edge of the bed, her thighs spread wide.

Amara played with her nipples as she looked down at them both. "Dear Lord, I am one lucky woman. Look at you two." She licked her lips. "I want you both. Now. Can we do that? Can you take me and make me come? Because if you don't hurry, I might just do it myself." With a wicked gleam in her eyes, she slowly slid her fingers down her belly and over her mound. When she flicked her clit ever so slightly, Seth had to hold the base of his dick so he didn't come right then.

He was already a virgin—not that they knew that—he didn't need to come early like an innocent.

Tristan stopped her hand and bit her inner thigh. "Bad, bad Amara. This is my pussy now. Mine and Seth's. We'll be the ones to make you come, darling."

With that, Tristan lowered his head and licked her. When she called out their names, Seth moved to kneel beside Tristan, wanting a taste of his own. He still had one hand on the base of his dick, but he ran the other down Tristan's back. The other man groaned and turned his head to capture Seth's lips.

Seth growled at the honey on Tristan's tongue. "She's so fucking sweet, and I love her taste on you, but I want to taste her for myself."

"Then do it," Tristan growled. "Fuck her with your tongue and eat up that sweet pussy. Make her ours, Seth."

Seth didn't wait any longer; he lowered his head and gently bit down on her clit. Amara's hand went to the back of his head and pressed him closer.

"Seth!" she called out, rocking her hips.

He licked her and nibbled on her outer lips before

dipping his tongue inside. He moved over slightly as Tristan joined him. They both ate her out, savoring their feast as their tongues brushed against one another.

"That is the hottest thing I've ever seen in my life," Amara panted. "Both of your heads between my thighs as you lick me and each other. I'm going to—" She didn't finish her sentence. Instead, she bucked once more, coming hard on their faces.

Seth lapped at her, wanting her to get to the edge again. She was beautiful when she came, pink and so fucking soft. As her body began to come down, Tristan moved away and tugged slightly on Seth's dick.

Seth grunted and kissed the other man. "Yeah?"

"Go up to the front of the bed make our girl feel loved," Tristan ordered. He looked down at Amara. "I'm going to fuck you, darling, then Seth will. Both of us won't be fully inside you at the same time for a while yet. You need to get used to us."

She nodded, her eyes dark with lust. "Good idea. You're both a little big for that right off the bat."

Tristan slapped her thigh. "You say the nicest things. Now turn over on that stomach of yours. I'm going to fuck you from behind while you suck Seth off right to the point of coming. You want him to come in your pussy, don't you?"

Amara pressed her thighs together and Seth once

again had to squeeze the base of his cock. "Hell, Tristan. You're a dirty talker."

"You know it. Now do as I say, darling, and I'll make you come again. And again." He winked, and Seth moved to the front of the bed while Amara rolled on her stomach.

They positioned themselves as they wanted so each of them was on the bed, and when Amara propped herself up on her hands and knees and slid her mouth over Seth's dick, he almost came again. Hell, if he weren't careful, he'd blow with just the gentle touch she had.

He slid his hands through her hair and gently rubbed her cheek with his thumb. "You okay, Amara?"

In answer, she hummed around his cock and took him deeper. Seth's eyes crossed and he leaned forward to roll her nipples between his fingertips. When she groaned around his dick, he sucked in a breath and met Tristan's eyes.

Tristan slowly worked his way in and out of Amara, his shoulders tense, but his motions reverent. The fae had his hands on her hips but moved them back and forth over her ass as he massaged her. The look of pure bliss on Tristan's face once again made Seth almost lose it.

When Tristan moved one hand down and over Amara's clit, Amara pulled back from Seth's cock and raised herself so her back was to Tristan's chest. Seth took her lips, kissing her for all he was worth, even as he worshiped her breasts. She came on Tristan's cock and their fae soon followed.

While Amara still shook, Tristan moved Seth ever so slightly. Seth ended up on his back with Amara on top of him. Tristan knelt beside them, his mouth on Amara's breasts and his fingers on her clit. Amara met Seth's eyes as she slowly lowered herself onto Seth's cock.

Seth gripped her hips and shook, his body aching for this, for her, for their fae, for *everything*. He'd never felt anything like her—so warm, so tight, so *her*. When she was fully seated, he swallowed hard and took one hand to tangle his fingers with hers. Tristan had his mouth and hands on them both while Amara began to move, her hand clasped with Seth's.

She rolled her hips, riding him while never breaking eye contact. He licked his lips, moving his own hips up to meet hers with each roll. When it was all too much and his balls couldn't tighten any more, Tristan seemed to understand and pinched her clit. Amara's cunt tightened around his cock and she came hard, sending Seth over the edge.

He filled her up, his body shaking to the point he knew he'd be sore the next morning. Tristan took Amara's lips, then Seth's, before pulling Amara down so she could take Seth's mouth.

Tristan ended up on his side with his arms wrapped around Seth and Amara, their breaths coming in pants.

Seth's heart ached, his body spent, but his mind whirling.

The bond hadn't snapped into place.

It hadn't worked.

Tears slid over Amara's cheeks and her body shook as she wept. Tristan held them both, silent but stoic. Seth couldn't speak, couldn't formulate the words for what this meant. Instead, he ran his hands over Amara's back and promised himself that he wouldn't let her leave them —bond or no.

When he finally opened his mouth to speak, Amara froze. Her body twisted one way then the other as she lifted her torso off him, her mouth open in a silent scream.

Tristan cursed and quickly sat up, bringing her into his arms. "She's changing," he bit out. "Fuck, I didn't know it would hurt her this bad."

Seth scrambled up and went to Amara's other side, holding her close, rocking her body back and forth.

"What does this mean?" he asked Tristan, who looked worried as hell.

"I don't know," he gasped. "I just don't fucking know."

Amara's body would only change to her paranormal half once she'd made love to her mate or mates. That's how the lightning-struck worked. Yet the bond hadn't come to be between the three of them.

It didn't make any sense.

Seth couldn't think about all of that yet. His mate, his Amara was in pain, and he couldn't fix it. Instead, he did his best to hold her close and prayed her agony would end soon.

What happened once she woke? Well...that was something they would have to figure out. Because something had happened, and it wasn't like the others.

When it came to the three of them, nothing seemed to be.

CHAPTER 4

Amara was dying. There was no other explanation for the fiery burn dancing along her skin and searing her down to her bones. She wanted to scream, but no matter what she did, no sound came out. It was like she was falling from a plane and moving too fast to let a shout escape.

Somehow, she could sense Tristan and Seth on either side of her, holding her close and whispering to her. However, they could be screaming at her for all she knew, she just couldn't hear it. All she knew was that it *hurt,* and she wanted whatever was happening to be over.

She'd been through hell before, had her bones broken and her face bruised. She'd had countless cuts and abrasions scattered over her body thanks to hands and fists belonging to those far larger than her. And yet, the agony dwelling within her now, cascading outside her, was even worse.

Her fingers curled and she lowered her head as another wave of fire crashed into her. She sucked in a breath, praying it would be over soon. Dimly, she remembered her friends explaining the pain and agony that had come with changing into their paranormal halves once they'd completed the mating bond.

Only there hadn't been a mating bond between her, Tristan, and Seth.

She'd cried for that in the short time the realization had taken to unfold, let the tears fall for a future that would never come to be.

And yet here she was, perhaps changing into something non-human altogether.

It didn't make any sense.

As quickly as it had come, the pain went away. She fell in a heap of limbs, yet her men—*her men*, dear goddess—caught her in their arms. They ran their hands up and down her sides and arms, kissing her softly on her temple and shoulders, as if they couldn't help but caress her. Her skin was so sensitive that their slight brushes felt so much deeper, so much more precise, but she wouldn't take away their touch for the world.

She didn't want to think about what that meant, or how she would deal once they spoke about their lack of bond.

"Amara," Tristan said softly. He brushed her hair back from her face before cupping her cheek. "Talk to me, darling. Does it still hurt? What can we do?"

"I..." She coughed, and Tristan looked over her head at Seth.

"Hold her," Tristan ordered before leaving her and Seth on the bed.

As Seth had already been holding her, he just brought her tightly to his chest and kissed her softly on the lips.

"You scared the hell out of me," he whispered. "I think Tristan is getting you water." He paused, and she looked up at him expectedly. "He doesn't really tell us everything he's doing as he'd doing it unless it's in bed."

She wanted to smile at that but she was too damned tired. "That's true. And we're going to have to fix that." She coughed again, and Seth ran his hands over her.

"Don't speak. Wait for Tristan to get you the water."

Even as he spoke, she felt her energy bouncing back, this time with a resurgence she didn't understand. It was almost as if nothing had happened. Yet she knew that wasn't the case. She'd purposely not looked at her skin or anything having to do with herself. What had changed? Was she still the same Amara as before, or had she shifted into something paranormal? And if she *had* changed, what did that mean?

She lay in the arms of one of the men she wanted to be hers in truth, yet she was too afraid to hope that with the possibility of her changing, fate would actually provide for her. It hadn't in the past, and she didn't want to think it could happen now. Hope only brought pain and disappointment. It was something she'd been taught at an early age, and it would take more than the idea of magic and fate to change that.

Tristan returned quickly, still naked but with a glass of water in his hand. Later, she'd scold him for allowing anyone else to see him naked as there were others in the home. He was hers and Seth's, only they got that right.

She gulped down the water and sighed once Tristan lifted it from her hands. "Thank you. I feel much better." She frowned. "In fact, I feel even better than I did before everything happened." She licked her lips. "*What* exactly happened?"

Tristan cupped her cheek even as Seth leaned closer. "You changed, Amara."

Apprehension slid over her skin. "What...what am I?"

"You're a siren, Amara." Tristan paused. "A fucking beautiful siren."

Images of mermaids and long-haired women luring sailors to their deaths filled her head and she frowned.

"There are *sirens*?"

Seth snorted. "Yeah, and you're one of them. Sirens and the merpeople have a long history, so you being one kind of rocks."

Amara's head hurt. Instead of saying anything, she

pulled away from both men and scrambled off the bed. They let her go but followed her to the mirror above the dresser. When she spotted her reflection, she paused.

"Dude."

Not the most eloquent of phrases, but honestly, she didn't know what else to say.

Because, *dude.*

Her skin glowed. Freaking glowed. And that wasn't even the fantastical part. Lavender and scarlet floral and script tattoos covered her sides and hips, going up and under her breasts before circling back to her shoulders and down her arms. The ink continued up the side of her neck and framed her face.

Her temples, the sides of her jaw, and up to part of her forehead with two branches coming out over her eyebrows and hairline also held the tattoos.

Normally, she'd have thought she looked, well, a little freaky, but for some reason, it felt...right.

Her eyes themselves hadn't been enlarged, but the brown of her irises had turned lavender, the color taking up even more area than before, as if the whites of her eyes had lessened.

She for sure wouldn't be able to walk down the street looking like this.

"Like with Nadie's ink from being a succubus, the script and colors come from what lineage you carry in your veins," Tristan said softly. His fingers trailed over her arm and she shivered. "I haven't seen this script in…" He trailed off.

"What are you saying?"

"I'm not sure," he answered. He lowered his head and brushed his lips over hers. "I need to go to the Court and see if what I'm thinking is right. Do you and Seth mind staying here for a bit?"

She blinked at his abruptness. "What do you mean? What are you going to ask, Tristan? What's going on?"

He shook his head and ran a hand through his hair. "I don't know. Something's pinging in the back of my head, like a memory I can't quite reach. I'm nine hundred years old, and sometimes I don't remember everything. Will you two wait here while I figure it out? I don't want to mention it in case it's nothing and I'm wrong, but I need to go."

"You're being vague and I'm not sure I like it," Seth put in. "But, if you need to go, then go. Just make sure you come back because we have a whole hell of a lot to deal with when you do. Okay?" With that, he kissed Tristan hard then moved out of the way for Amara.

She folded her arms over her stomach, aware they were all still naked and they hadn't talked about what they'd just done together, or what her changing meant in terms of the lack of bond between them. However, if Tristan felt this was important, she would have to trust him. Trust, in general, didn't come easily to her, but she would try.

"Come back soon," she said then kissed his jaw. He lowered his head and took her mouth in a passionate kiss before he pulled away. "I'll be back soon." He sighed, looking distracted, then grabbed his clothes from the floor and headed back out of the room.

Both she and Seth watched him walk away.

"You know, he might annoy me with the way he doesn't tell us his thoughts, but damn that man can walk away like no other," Seth said with a groan. "That ass? Seriously."

Despite the tension and uncertainty filling her, Amara laughed and leaned into Seth. "That he can. And your ass is pretty nice, too." She reached around and pinched him, loving the gasp that sounded. "What do you say we find some robes or one of his shirts to put on and grab something to eat in this big place? I'm suddenly starving."

She ran a hand over her temple and the ink seemed to pulsate under her fingers. She was a siren, a mythical creature that, apparently, wasn't so mythical. What that meant in the long run, she didn't know, but if she didn't take it one step at a time, she'd freak out beyond reason.

"I can probably scent our way to the kitchen," Seth said as he pulled on his jeans, leaving the waist unbuttoned. He held out his shirt. "How about you put this on so we don't go through his things." He blushed a bit and shrugged. "I know we just slept together and all, but since he didn't actually give us a tour…"

She nodded, fully understanding his hesitation, and pulled Seth's shirt over her head. Since she was so much smaller than them both, the shirt billowed to the middle of her thighs. It covered enough of her, and frankly, she was too hungry to be modest. If she happened to meet up with any of the people who were inside Tristan's home, she'd deal with it then.

Amara took Seth's hand, and they made their way down the large staircase. Instead of turning left toward the sitting room, they went right. The scent of cooked meat and bread filled her nose, and she knew they were going in the right direction. Her stomach rumbled, and Seth chuckled.

"Let's get you fed."

As soon as they entered the large kitchen she blinked. A door on the other side swung closed, leaving her and Seth alone.

"It's like they don't want to be in the same room as us," she said dryly.

Seth just shrugged once again. "They haven't been introduced to us, and since Tristan is royalty, there might be some protocol or something. I don't think his family lives here since the place feels only of Tristan's energy and not another high-ranking fae, but I could be wrong."

She frowned as he went to the fridge and opened it.

"You can sense those sorts of things? Is that what mermen do?"

He pulled out two plates and lifted his brows. "It seems they made us plates since there's a third in there for Tristan." He wiggled one. "They have our names on it. They must have just stuck them in here because they're still hot."

They indeed had their names written on top of the foil with marker. She couldn't help but feel touched and a little out of her element. She'd never had anything like this. The kitchen itself was larger than her apartment with two six-top ranges and two dishwashers and refrigerators. The island in the middle was a piece of artwork, and she wanted to lay prostrate at Tristan's feet just so she would be able to cook in the room.

Her stomach rumbled again and she suddenly didn't care about the differences between her and the men she'd given herself to and wanted to eat whatever was on the plate.

"Anyway," Seth continued as he pulled off the foil to reveal still-hot roast beef, potatoes, green beans, corn, stuffing, and rolls. "First, I am hungry enough to eat my entire plate worth of food and possibly lick up whatever's left. Let's get forks. Second, as mermen, our powers are more about what we can do within water. The ability to sense other supernaturals is inherent in *every* supernatural. You'll be able to gauge another's presence and perhaps their power level too once we figure out your powers and you practice. First, though, we'll have to teach you to glamour so you don't end up showing up in the human realm with that lovely ink of yours."

Her eyes widened and her hand went to her temple, to the ink that felt natural even if it was brand new. "I forgot for a second. My brain isn't working. How could I just *not* think about what others will see when they look at me now."

Seth pulled the foil off her plate and procured two forks from a drawer in the island, after some searching around. "It's to be expected. Just breathe and eat—though not at the same time. That's all you need to do right now. Between the three of us *and* the other women's experiences when they changed and found their mates, we'll figure it out."

She took the fork and sat on one of the stools at the island, careful to sit on Seth's shirttail rather than just her naked butt. Some things should not be done in the kitchen, even if it might sound sexy.

As soon as she took the first bite of roast and gravy, she almost orgasmed again. Seth must have noticed, but he was too busy tearing through his food to comment. She did the same, getting through a good quarter of the plate before she looked up again. Seth had apparently put a glass of water in front of her and she was grateful.

"Sorry for zoning out. But, food."

He grinned at her and finished up his water before going back for more. "No problem. I did the same thing."

When he gulped half the glass in one go, she raised her brow. Something clicked about him and she wanted to know if what she'd thought was right. "You need water to survive, don't you?"

He nodded before taking another bite of food. She did the same, only this time, they were both a little slower since their appetite was at least somewhat sated.

"Yes. If I dry out, I die. Each realm, each species, has their own weaknesses and that is one of mine. As for everything else? I'm not exactly like you and Tristan when it comes to looking human. Tristan uses glamour to hide the slight luminescence of his skin and his pointed ears, and you will do the same to your ink and skin. I'm a shifter, so I don't use glamour. I actually just shift from one form to the other."

Her eyes widened. "I'd never thought of that."

He grinned and held out his leg. "See? No tail. I have a tail in my other form, and my skin sometimes has a gold or green sheen depending on the lighting. But it's only in places, and only when I'm fully shifted. It's like when wolves, bears, or dragons shift. They go from one form to another, depending." He grinned. "That also means, like the other shifters, we don't have sex in our mer form. That is only for the human form."

She choked on her roll and gulped water to wash it

down. "How on earth did you know I'd thought about that?" Even if it hadn't been a fully conscious thought.

He snorted. "Because everyone does. They want to know how a merman or mermaid can have sex with a tail in the way. We don't. We shift to human just like the other shifters do. It's not that complicated once you think about it, but most people just want to make fish jokes."

She laughed despite herself and shook her head. "I'm sorry, then."

Seth waved her off and continued eating. "It's no worry. This way you know. When we make love, I'll look like I do now."

She heated just thinking about it. First things first, though. "And when do I get to see your other form?"

Seth frowned. "It's not safe for me to shift without a body of water near. I lose too much energy in the process and I'm not as strong. I don't know if Tristan has a pool around and I'm not about to play rubber ducky in the bathtub."

"But you'd make bath time so much fun," she said with a grin.

He threw his head back and laughed before jumping off the stool and pulling her into his arms. He kissed her senseless and the laughter died, a heated tension and need replacing it.

"I'll show you once we go to my realm," he said softly. "How's that?"

"I think I like that idea," she whispered.

"I can't believe I waited so long," he said so quietly she almost missed it.

She narrowed her eyes. "Waited so long for what? To get me alone?"

He met her gaze and swallowed hard. "No. Ugh...I actually meant... Well, crap." He blushed hard, his ears turning red, and she saw the youth in him. He might be older than her, but he was far younger than most immortals. "I was a virgin before earlier. I mean, I've done things. Been with men and women, but I'd never fully had sex before now. At first, it was because I was training to be a warrior, and then because I seemed to be waiting for you and Tristan to show up. I'm sorry I didn't tell you, but it never seemed the right time, and I didn't want to pressure you into worrying about me when it was my choice in the first place. You know?"

She blinked. "How...how could you keep something like that from us? What the hell?" She pressed her lips together; hurt filling her for a moment before she pushed it away. This was about Seth, not her. "Oh, Seth, I wish I would have known." She cupped his face and he lowered his head toward her.

"I wanted it to be with you two, and it was special because it was us. I didn't need it to be even more so because it already was."

She shook her head, unable to think straight. "When

Tristan comes back, we should talk about it because he deserves to know. But Seth, don't keep things from us from now on. Okay?"

He kissed her softly in answer, and she sighed. Being with two men was more than hot sex, she knew that, but damn if she knew what she was doing. *One day at a time,* she reminded herself. Just one day at a time.

Seth pulled back and licked his lips. "Are you still hungry?" From the look in his eyes, she had a feeling he wasn't talking about just food anymore.

"I think we should go back up to the bedroom and get to know each other more," she said teasingly. She would have thought she was a succubus instead of a siren from they way her body craved.

Seth's eyes darkened and he took her lips once more. "Let's clean up before I make up for lost time."

She smiled and reached around to grab his ass. When he rocked toward her, she had to pull away so she could find some semblance of control.

"I'm not doing it in a kitchen," she said dryly. "Sorry."

Seth winked then moved to start cleaning up. The two of them did their dishes side by side and left them in the drying rack. Sure, there might be literal cleaning fairies around the home, but she didn't feel comfortable letting them do everything. She wasn't even fully comfortable in her own skin yet, let alone in Tristan's royal life.

When they made their way back into Tristan's

bedroom, Amara ran her hands over the shirt she wore, suddenly nervous. Seth stood in front of her and lifted her chin with his knuckle.

"What's wrong?" he asked, his voice soft.

"I'm suddenly nervous," she whispered. "I mean, before it was the three of us..."

He visibly winced. "And you only want to make love when it's the three of us?" When he moved to pull back, she gripped his wrist, keeping him in place.

"No," she said firmly. "That is not what I meant. I'm going about this all wrong. Before, when it was the three of us, it was different because we were not only coming together for the first time, we were hoping the bond would come. And it didn't." She wouldn't let the tears fall from her eyes, but they wanted to.

Seth cupped her face and lowered his lips to hers, giving her a gentle kiss. "You changed into a siren, Amara. We *are* your mates. The bond might not have worked the first time, but it could still happen."

She raised a brow, trying to add levity to the situation. "You're saying we should just keep having sex to see what comes up."

He snorted then reached around her to cup her ass. "Well, I think we should keep having sex period. You *know* what's already come up." He rocked against her, his hard cock pressing into her belly. "And once Tristan comes back, we'll see why things are taking longer than they should. Until then, live in the moment, be with me."

I can do that, Amara thought sadly. She could push away the pain like she always did and try to find the good. And Seth was good. He was far more than anything she'd dreamt of. The light in his eyes, the way he tried to make things better even if it hurt to do so. She could and would fall in love with this man, just as she could and would fall in love with Tristan.

And if she lived in the moment, she could maybe find the happiness that had been denied her for so long.

Instead of saying any of that, she leaned forward and kissed him. Hard. When he moaned, massaging her ass with his large hands, she pressed her body more firmly into his.

His hands slid under the hem of the shirt and he cupped her more firmly, his fingers playing in the crease of her ass. When they dipped near her center, she spread her legs, wanting him to touch her deeper. Seth kept his lips on hers, possessively kissing her even as he slid his fingers in and out of her, running the pad of his middle finger over her clit with each pass.

When he curled them and hit her in that magical spot inside, she gasped, throwing her head back. Seth latched on to her neck instead, the sensation of his lips on her ink sending bolts of electric heat over her skin. He continued to fuck her with his fingers, first two, then three, before going for four. She had one leg over his hip, and he sped up, the sound of their panting and his fingers moving through her wetness echoing in the room. When he moved even harder, she sucked in a breath, her back bowing. She came with a shout and her body clenched around him.

Before she could fully come down from her high, Seth had her on her back on the bed and her shirt off. He'd also shucked his pants as he hovered over her. He crushed his mouth to hers then thrust into her in one hard stroke.

They both froze as soon as he was fully seated, their bodies shaking as she stretched to accommodate him.

"Fuck me," she panted. "Make me yours."

Seth licked his lips, his shoulders straining as he held himself back. "I've never tried this position you know."

She grinned and pulled one leg high so it rested on his shoulder. The other she wrapped around his waist. The position forced him to go deeper and they both gasped.

"Don't worry, honey," she said on a sigh. "I'll take care of you. Now fuck me."

She cupped her breasts and he *moved*.

He thrust in and out of her with a vigor that nearly sent her over the edge once again. It took a minute for him to find his rhythm, but when he did, she had to cling to his shoulder with one hand so she could stay firmly in the middle of the bed. Her hips lifted, meeting him thrust for thrust, even as he latched on to one nipple with his mouth. He laved at her then went to the other one, never once pausing his motions.

Once he lifted his head, she met his gaze and licked her lips. He kissed her then, even as he slid one hand between them. The action forced her leg on his shoulder to tighten as he leaned on that arm, but it only made her want to come. His fingers slid over her clit, already wet from her arousal. With that one touch, she shattered, her pussy squeezing him like a vice. He soon followed, filling her up so hard she could feel the hot seed deep within her.

He shouted her name even as she did the same with his. He kept moving, though, his body never quitting. She thought she'd pass out from the way her body had already climaxed, but, apparently, they weren't through.

He lowered her legs so she was fully flat on her back and he rocked himself in and out of her, in and out. He met her gaze, one arm keeping him steady above her, the other moving to graze her body, then cup her face.

"Come again, Amara. Come for me."

She'd never thought Seth would ask that of her and expect her to do so, but just his sexy voice and the way he felt deep within her made her come again. This time not quite as hard, but rather soft and slowly. The ache slid over her body like a wave, tingling through her nipples and over her neck.

Lazily, she wrapped one arm around him and cupped his cheek with her free hand. "Mine," she whimpered, not knowing why she would say that right then.

"Yours, my sweetling. Yours forever." He kissed her, this time slow and wanting. "As you're mine."

When he pulled away, tears slid down her cheeks, and he kissed them one by one until she found herself weeping in his arms, both of them on their sides as she tried to understand why fate had decreed him and Tristan hers yet wouldn't allow her to have what came with it.

Seth kissed her temple and held her close. "Sleep, Amara. We'll bond, my siren. I promise."

She wanted to believe him, wanted to know it was true. She let herself drift off, and when the bed dipped slightly and the spicy scent of Tristan filled her senses, she let herself sleep fully in the arms of her men.

Amara would never let them go, even if there weren't a bond. That was what she vowed to herself right then. She'd fight for this, fight for them. They were worth it. And with the way they looked at her, she was just starting to figure out that she was worth it, as well.

CHAPTER 5

Tristan held a sleeping Amara in his arms and met Seth's gaze. It seemed he'd missed a few things, but he knew that they needed time as a couple as he and Amara would. As he and Seth would.

He let out a breath and sank deeper into the pillow.

"You okay?" Seth mouthed, and Tristan nodded slightly.

He looked down at the sleeping woman in his arms and back up at the merman who already held a part of his heart. "Later," he mouthed back.

As soon as Seth closed his eyes, Tristan did the same and fell asleep, despite the events of the day. Trepidation skittered over his skin as well as uneasiness as to what he'd discovered at Court, but he would talk about it with the others in the morning.

They would also have to travel soon. While he had wanted to show Amara his realm and take his time, it seemed they, like the other lightning-struck before her, would have to be on the run.

When he woke up, the others were still sleeping and he quietly slipped out of bed. While he'd have liked to wake them up in his own special way, as well as share a shower with them, he knew he didn't have that kind of time. Instead, he padded toward the bathroom and took a quick shower on his own. As soon as he got out, his phone started to buzz and he cursed.

He answered quickly and whispered on his way out of the bedroom, thankful the others were still sleeping soundly. "Malik?"

"Hey," the other man said, his voice oddly deep. Tristan would have asked the lion shifter what was wrong, but Malik was notoriously private. "Why are you whispering?"

"I had to walk by a sleeping Seth and Amara. Why are you calling so early?"

The other man let out a long sigh. "It's good that you're with them. I'm happy for you."

For some reason, Tristan knew there was more to those words, but he let it go for now.

"Anyway, the reason I'm calling is that I've heard rumblings about your siren."

Tristan froze. He'd called Malik the day before as

soon as he'd seen Amara's ink because Malik had a decent knowledge base about lineages in realms. The lion hadn't recognized it then, but that didn't mean he hadn't heard something. Tristan had also gone to the Court to discreetly ask around about the same thing, and yet there were already rumblings.

This couldn't be good.

"What have you heard?"

"It's not much, but there's a split in the siren realm right now. The current royal line isn't in favor and hasn't been for a long time. Apparently, they also felt the presence of a new siren in their midst."

"Fuck."

"Pretty much. Just be careful. I'll find out what I can about her lineage, but you know who you need to talk to."

Tristan sighed. "I know, and we'll be seeing her today."

"Good. And stay safe, Tristan."

"Thank you, Malik." He ended the call and let out a curse. Of course, when he found his mate things would go to shit. He just figured they'd have a little longer to deal with it. Apparently not.

"Tristan?"

He turned at the sound of Amara coming toward him, her body covered in Seth's shirt from the previous day. While he wanted to see her in his shirt one day, the sight of her in Seth's just made him rock-hard.

"Did I wake you?" he asked, even as he opened his arms. She came to him quickly, wrapping her arms around his waist. It surprised him how quickly this had become normal, the feel of her in his arms and by his side. He'd do anything to keep it that way.

"No, it was time for me to wake up anyway. Seth is up, too." She stood on her tiptoes and traced her fingers along his jaw. "What's worrying you?"

He lowered his head and kissed her softly, the minty taste of toothpaste telling him she'd borrowed one of the spare toothbrushes he'd left on the sink. He hadn't given her any time to pack before bringing her to his realm, and now, he'd be bringing her to another realm without her things.

"Once Seth gets out here, we can talk."

"I'm here," Seth said as he made his way toward them, dressed only in the jeans he'd had on the day before. "What's going on?"

Tristan sighed and took both of their hands. They stood in the hallway of his home, and yet he didn't want to move them to a more comfortable space as he needed to get through things quickly so they could leave at once.

"I went to the fae Court to ask a few people some questions. The ink on your skin was nagging me." Amara's eyes narrowed and he quickly shook his head. "Not because it's not beautiful. I meant because I felt like I'd seen it before. And I might have, but it was so long ago, I can't remember correctly. So I went to those in the Court who study such things, and while I was being vague, was told I needed to talk to someone who studies lineage."

Seth's eyes filled with understanding. "You mean Calypso?"

"Seth's sister?" Amara asked.

"Seth's sister," Tristan answered with a nod. "She studies lineage in depth, right?"

Seth nodded quickly. "Yeah, it's her role as a Conclave member, and now it's sort of an obsession. You're saying she'll be able to tell us what line Amara is from? Why is that important?"

"I don't know," Tristan said. "I don't know why it's important. Yet. I just know it is. And it's bugging me that I can't remember. And while we're discussing you, Amara, there's something else."

"What is it?" she asked as Seth tucked her to his side.

He told them about what Malik had said about the siren royal line and what problems may come of that, and Amara visibly sagged.

"Nothing is ever easy, is it?" she asked then shook her head. "Between what I've turned into and what it might mean and the fact that the bond didn't come…it's just too much."

A pang twisted in Tristan's heart at the last part, and he let out a breath. "We'll figure it out."

"We keep saying that," she said softly.

"And it's been a day," Seth added. "I take it we're heading to my realm soon, then? Since people are already talking about Amara becoming a siren, I have a feeling we should figure out what's triggering your memory ASAP."

Tristan nodded. "Something tells me we need to move quickly." He brought both of them into his arms, the feeling as if it had been forever and yet not long enough all at once. "I have clothes for Amara," he said once they pulled away. "My staff picked up a few items in your size since we never brought your own things."

"We didn't really plan out what we were going to do," Amara said dryly. "I sort of just took a big leap."

"And I, for one, am glad you leapt," he said softly then took her lips. He did the same to Seth before pulling away and pushing them to get what they needed so they could leave quickly.

As it was Seth's realm they were going to, the other man would be the one to open the portal. Tristan could do it easily, but since he wasn't sure exactly where Calypso lived, it would be better for Seth to work it out.

"Now we're going to go through the portal and end up on the outside of the inner wards," Seth explained. "I can get us into the outer wards easily, but Amara, since you've never been there before, I'll have to swim you to where you can easily walk around."

Her eyes widened and Tristan grinned. "Do I need to hold my breath? I feel like your realm is much different than the others."

"It is, but I'll help you. Before we go, I'll give each of you the Kiss of Life. That will allow you to breathe under water for the short time it takes for me to swim you to where there are air pockets that you can walk around in. We have giant domes on our ocean floor, as well as scattered throughout the sea where many of our buildings are. I can live just as easily with my fin as I can with my feet, but we do have non-merpeople who live with us, either mated in or otherwise. That and other various reasons led to the building of the domes."

Amara leaned into Tristan, her eyes wide. "Okay...so you're going to kiss me, then push me through a portal where we'll end up in the ocean. Then you'll have your fin and swim Tristan and me to where we can breathe normally without magic and walk around?"

Seth smiled before kissing her forehead. "Yep. I know it sounds crazy, but it's how we work. Faith and Levi have both been through it." He winced. "Though we didn't know they were in the water until almost too late. You, however, will be able to breathe easily in normal air and in water as soon as I kiss you."

"And what if it runs out."

Seth's mouth set. "It won't. I'll be with you at all times.

And as my mates—bond or no—the others won't touch you. I'm a warrior and protect what is mine."

Tristan couldn't help but fill with pride at the way Seth spoke of them. Each of the three came from such different worlds, and yet together, they had the experiences to make their lives whole. He'd never thought too deeply as to whom he would mate—he'd always been scared he'd be disappointed. Never once would he have thought that he'd be with a merman and a siren. Such perfection in their dichotomy, yet two halves of his whole.

And once he found a way to create the bond in truth, he'd have his fate.

"Ready?" Seth asked, not a lick of worry in his tone. He would protect them, of that Tristan was sure.

"I trust you," Amara answered, and Tristan knew those words were tough for her. He might not know everything about her past—and one day he would—but that much he knew.

Tristan nodded and licked his lips before Seth kissed him. This was no ordinary kiss. While their tongues collided and he wanted to rub up against the other man, the magic between them flared. Warmth spread over him, and he knew that whatever Seth was doing was working.

Seth moved back, patted Tristan's cheek, then moved to kiss Amara. She didn't look as sure as she had a moment ago but fell into Tristan's arms anyway. Once again, magic pulsated within the room as Amara was given the Kiss of Life.

When Seth pulled back again, he grinned and took their hands. "Ready?"

"As I'll ever be," Amara said. She might sound nervous, but she was brave as hell for doing all she'd done.

In a blink, Tristan found himself in the middle of the ocean, fighting for breath. Only he didn't have to fight. He could breathe easily, and he'd only freaked out because it was so new. He turned to Amara, who was in Seth's arms. Her eyes were wide and her mouth worked, but with Seth's help, she looked as if she was doing okay. Apparently, the Kiss of Life also made it easier for him to see in the depths of the ocean in this realm. Good thing, since he desperately wanted to see Seth's other form.

The man was a god.

At least, he looked like one.

He'd always been ripped, but with the water surrounding him, he looked even more so. His long, blue-green tail swished as he kept the three of them steady. It shined within the depths of the water and looked strong as hell. It was longer than his legs so he had to be at least seven feet now. His skin had taken on a gold hue, and when he moved, Tristan was sure he saw blue-green glitter or scales.

How extraordinary.

They couldn't speak underwater, but Seth met their

gazes, took their hands, and nodded. Before Tristan could think about what they were doing, Seth began to swim.

And holy hell could the man move.

He pulled Tristan and Amara toward a bright light, and Tristan could only marvel at Seth's powers. He knew Seth was young and still growing in magic, and one day, the man would rival any leader. Tristan couldn't wait for that.

Before he could truly enjoy the ride, though, they came upon an ancient underground castle. Seth pushed through a barrier and Tristan found himself wet and coughing on his ass while Amara leaned against Seth, catching her breath.

Tristan raised a brow at Seth, who shrugged.

"Sorry for the rough landing," his lover said with a shy smile. "I'm not used to hauling two people through the border like that. I'll get it down eventually." He held out his hand and helped Tristan to his feet. The other man now stood on two legs, rather than a tail, and he even had his jeans on. How merfolk could do that, he didn't know, but it was a handy gift.

"That was..." Amara said softly then shook her head. "That was *awesome*." She smiled wide as she ran her hands over her wet clothes. "We're going to have to do that again. And I'm going to need a towel."

Seth kissed her temple while he squeezed Tristan's hand. "We can get you a towel at my sister's."

"Will she be at home, then?" Tristan asked. Calling ahead between realms didn't always work. In fact, it rarely worked at all. Most places were even on a different linear plane, meaning that time moved differently. They had to be careful how long they stayed in one place if they were planning to meet anyone. In reality, it was only a few moments off between realms for most places. However, the difference between the hell realm and the rest of them was the most significant. Hence, why it was called hell. Well, that and the demons, fire, and lava.

"I'm here, actually," Calypso said as she made her way toward them. She looked like Seth, her long, chestnut hair hanging in waves down her back and over her shoulders. She was only a few inches shorter, as well; which meant she was pretty damn tall. "We don't have time to waste," she said quickly. "Let's go to my place." She looked over her shoulder at the people milling about in human form and the others in mer form in the water surrounding the castle. "Now."

There was a reason Calypso was a Conclave member, and the immense power radiating from her was only part of it. She had to be at least a century or two older than Seth, as well; but looked the same age as immortals never looked too far past their prime.

Seth brushed a kiss to her forehead then pulled Amara close to him. "Let's go, then. Introductions later."

Amara nodded, and Tristan did as well as they followed Calypso to her home. He assumed she had more than one as he figured not everyone wanted to live in the hustle and bustle of the underwater city at all times, but this was the one they were meeting at. Since Seth had brought them here, this one must be the one she lived at most often.

Tristan was overthinking and worried about his mates. Since the bond hadn't snapped into place and Amara and Seth weren't his in truth as of yet, he couldn't quite think clearly. His heart hurt, and he needed to push that away if he wanted to figure out the next step. As long as he was cool and logical, he would figure it out.

Amara leaned into him and he knew then that there would be no clear and logical when it came to his feelings for her...or Seth.

He shook his head, trying to clear his thoughts of what could happen and focus on what was more important at that moment. They made their way into Calypso's place and he glanced around at the elegant home but couldn't focus. There was something going on that he couldn't quite figure out, and hopefully, Seth's sister would be able to help.

"So, I take it the bond didn't come?" Calypso asked bluntly. He'd always admired the way his fellow Conclave member spoke, but right then, he wanted her to use a little more finesse.

Tristan looked over at Amara, but his mate—yes, *mate*, despite the lack of bond—merely raised her chin.

"No, there is no bond," Amara answered, her voice cool. "You're Seth's sister, then? You'll be able to tell us why? Or at least point us in the right direction."

Calypso sighed and shook her head. "I'm sorry. I'm so damn sorry. I had hoped what I'd been hearing and what I thought might be happening was wrong, but it seems I'm not. Yes, Amara, I'm Calypso, Seth's sister. Again, I'm sorry for not introducing myself properly, but there isn't much time."

Tristan fisted his hands. "What are you saying?"

"Stop with the cryptic bullshit, Caly," Seth said. "Amara and I aren't Conclave members so you don't have to hide your true meaning when you speak."

Tristan narrowed his eyes but didn't say anything. It was true he'd had to double-speak in the past to survive and keep his people alive, but a Conclave member wasn't all he was.

"Take a seat," Calypso said as she gestured toward the couches. "The sirens are on the brink of war, and many don't even seem to understand it. The queen has been in power for far too long. And while we are all long-lived, practically immortal, usually there is some sort of way for the powers at large to change over when the realm is falling apart. However, this queen," Caly shook her head, "this queen is using curses, fear, and death in order to stay in power. As sirens, you can sing to souls."

Amara sucked in a breath. "What does that mean?"

"It means different things for different clans, but you are from the Windwalker clan." Caly shook her head. "Don't ask how I know, just know I know. It's part of who I am. The Windwalker clan was banished centuries ago. Cursed by the queen. Your clan can sing to souls, and by doing that, they can go past merely joining with another soul for that time being, they can bring that soul to life...or to death."

Tristan brought Amara to his lap at those words, knowing she would need to be held. Seth held her hand and slid over so his thigh pressed hard against Tristan's.

"It's a powerful gift," Tristan whispered and kissed her temple. "But you can control it." For some reason, he knew that was one reason she shook, her fear of lack of control, and as soon as he'd said the words, she calmed fractionally.

"Tell me what else," Amara said softly, yet strong. "Tell me why the Windwalkers were banished."

"You were too powerful," Calypso said simply. "The queen was afraid she'd lose power so she cursed those who were to come and killed anyone she could. Your clan was not allowed to bond. No matter how close they came to one another as true mates, they could never feel the pull. The queen slowly but methodically killed off the rest of the clan, and no one else was strong enough to do anything about it. You see, she *broke* the existing bonds." Caly's voice broke, and Seth reached out to grip his sister's hands. "I don't know how she did it, but she did. I didn't think it was possible."

"Why haven't we heard of this?" Tristan asked. "Why didn't the Conclave do anything about it?"

Calypso cursed under her breath. "Oh, some knew. And those who knew are dead now. I didn't find out until recently, and I've been trying to deal with what I could. It's not my realm, though, Tristan, and as soon as I heard Amara was a siren, I did what I could."

"You're the messenger," Amara said sharply. "We won't hurt you or hate you for your words. Now, how do we lift the curse so I can be with my mates? I don't want anything to do with the queen. I don't have powers…or rather I don't know how to use them so I'm not going to go for her throne. I just want to be with Tristan and Seth and go back to Dante's Circle and live my life. I just want a *home*."

There was something in her words that made Tristan pause, a deep pain he knew he would have to find out the cause of, but then he thought more of the threat.

"The queen knows," Tristan said, his voice hollow. "The queen knows another of the line she fought to eradicate is here, and that's why everyone is being so hush-

hush. That's why people don't know what's going on because they only have parts of the whole story."

Calypso nodded.

"What does this mean? And how the hell do we break the curse?" Amara asked, her voice rising.

"You can only break the curse by getting the one who laid it to take it off." Caly paused, met Tristan's eyes, then Seth's, then Amara's. "The curse must be lifted in life...or in death."

Tristan cursed again, and Seth let out a small growl.

"And from the sound of this queen, she's not going to let me off easily." Amara leaned into Tristan's hold and he ran his hand up and down her arm. "I...I don't want to have to kill someone. I know I'm not exactly new to the world of the paranormal even though I'm new to *my* world and the way things must be, but...I don't know if I can do that."

Seth leaned into them both and kissed her brow, then Tristan's. "We'll figure it out."

"You'll have to," Callypso added. "Because the queen of the sirens won't take no for an answer. She'll do all in her power to regain control. There's a reason the sirens have been so quiet on the Conclave and in other realm matters. They have their own pain and strife to deal with, their own queen to cower to. But that won't last for long. The queen will want more power in some way, and she will break through the realms to get it. They say the sirens called men to their deaths, and yet that's only a fraction of it. Don't take this lightly, Seth. Don't let them out of your sight, Tristan. Because no matter what, it will take the three of you on the siren's door for you to find what you need."

Calypso's voice had gone into a song of its own as she spoke, her eyes wide and glassy. At her words, Seth had jumped off the couch and caught her as she fell into his arms. She shook her head and pushed him away.

"I'm fine," she said, her voice a rasp. She closed her eyes and rubbed her temples. "I just need some tea and a bath."

"You're a prophet," Tristan said, surprised. It took a lot to surprise him these days, but since he'd met Amara, nothing had been the same.

Caly shrugged one shoulder. "Maybe. I don't know. If I did, maybe I wouldn't be here." With that odd statement, she patted her brother's cheek and walked away. "You're welcome to the cottage in the back. I know you'll need your rest before you head to the siren realm."

"Your sister is something else," Amara said with awe in her voice. Tristan agreed.

"She's always just been my sister," Seth said with a frown. "I've never known her any other way." He turned to Tristan and Amara. "We should take her up on that cottage. Get some rest. Try to figure out what to do next. For some reason, I don't think we have much time."

Tristan stood up and set Amara on her feet. "I think you're right."

"And to think, I thought my life was boring," Amara said.

Tristan cupped her face and kissed her softly. "You've never been boring."

"You didn't know me before."

"I know you now, and I want to know you more."

Seth cleared his throat and stood by their sides. He didn't say anything, but he didn't need to. They were all on the same page. Their lives had changed and things had gone to hell, but they were together. That part had to matter. Because if it didn't...well, Tristan didn't want to think about what would happen if it all fell apart.

He might be a fae with powers that were the highest order of his realm, but broken, he wouldn't be able to face another century—not without Amara, without Seth. Not without his future.

CHAPTER 6

S eth watched Amara sleep, knowing she had to be exhausted. The change had taken its toll on her, and he knew all the news about bonds, fate, curses and her realm hadn't helped. Only a couple of days had passed, and yet his world, *their* world had altered completely. Since he sat next to her on the bed, he brushed a long strand of hair away from her face and just stared at her.

He'd never thought to be so lucky as to have a mate like her, let alone another mate like Tristan. He didn't know all of their secrets or how they liked their coffee or any other odd details like that, but he'd learn them. What mattered most was that the three of them were committed to each other and to finding a way to make the bond work. It wasn't exactly the way he'd thought he would mate, but he'd take it as it was.

He didn't want to think about what would happen when they reached the siren realm. The queen sounded like a piece of work, and he'd be damned if he'd force Amara to do something so against her nature in order for their bond to snap into place. Calypso hadn't said anything about *Amara* being the one to end the queen's life. She'd only said that the queen would need to break the curse on her own—or die—to have the curse fall apart.

Amara had only heard that the queen would have to die and had put that responsibility on herself. Seth—and he was sure Tristan, as well—would be damned if they broke Amara's spirit in the process of breaking the curse.

A hand came down on his shoulder, and he looked up at Tristan. He hadn't sensed the other man approach as he'd been so focused on Amara and their next steps.

Tristan lifted his chin toward the door, and Seth nodded. He quickly placed a kiss on Amara's lips, though she didn't stir, and stood up. Tristan leaned over and kissed her as well before taking Seth's hand and leading him toward the door. They walked the hallway in silence, their fingers entwined, and Seth's heartbeat pounded in his ears. He'd been alone with Tristan before, of course, but this was different. He could sense the anticipation in the air and his skin tingled as if the slightest touch would set him off. He took a deep breath as they made their way to one of the open pools in Calypso's home and tried to calm himself. He, like the others, had a thousand things on his mind, and being with Tristan like he wanted shouldn't have been at the forefront.

But it was.

He wanted the man at his side, wanted him against his body, wanted him in his mouth, in *him*.

"You're thinking too hard," Tristan said from his side. "You and Amara share that trait."

Seth turned to his mate and tilted his head. He studied Tristan's face, his gaze tracing the softness of his lips, the high cheekbones, the brightness of his eyes. Tristan hadn't put on his glamour so his ears were pointed, his skin carrying that luminescence that spoke of age-old power.

"You think just as hard, Tristan," Seth finally said, his voice low. "If not harder."

Tristan cupped Seth's face and leaned forward. "Then let's not think at all for now. Amara is asleep, and we aren't heading out of the mer realm for a little while. Let's just *be*." He kissed Seth then, his lips firm yet yielding.

Seth moaned into him before he wrapped his arms around Tristan's waist. The long lines of their bodies melded together, their hard cocks pressed against one another. Tristan let out a throaty groan and deepened the kiss. His lover's fingers tugged on Seth's hair and pulled, the action forcing Seth's head to the side. He rocked his cock into Tristan's as the fae's lips latched on to his neck, sucking and licking until they were both squirming against one another.

Tristan pulled back, his pupils wide and his breaths uneven. "I want you, Seth. I know your first time was with Amara and myself, and then you were with her once more, but will you be with me alone? Will you let me fuck you?" He paused. "And you're lucky we haven't had time to dwell on the fact that you and Amara told me after the fact you were a virgin."

Seth swallowed hard and nodded. "I want you, Tristan. I want you in me in every way, and I want to be in you." He paused. "Unless that's not something you like."

Tristan traced his thumb along Seth's cheekbone. "I like many things, but with you Seth, I like *all* the things. But first, I want your mouth on me. These lips?" He slid this thumb over Seth's lips before sinking it into Seth's mouth. Seth sucked, and Tristan groaned. "Yes, these lips. I want them wrapped around my cock like you're wrapped around my thumb. You want that, Seth? You want me to fuck your face while you suck my cock?"

Seth sucked harder before releasing Tristan's thumb with a pop. "I want that, damn it. But..." He paused then grinned. "But I'm going to show you something I've always wanted to do *while* I suck your cock." He reached between them and squeezed. Tristan's eyes crossed and Seth grinned. "Take off your pants and get in the pool."

Tristan's eyes widened and the fae threw his head

back and laughed. "I forgot mermen could breathe underwater even without their tail."

Seth licked his lips. "Ever have an underwater blowjob before?"

Tristan shook his head. "Hell no, but I'm glad you'll be my first."

At those words, Seth felt the tips of his ears heat but he ignored it. "Just so you know, I've given blowjobs before, so I'm not all that innocent."

Tristan gripped the back of Seth's head and crushed his mouth to his. The fae gave him a brutal kiss before pulling back but not letting go of Seth's hair. "Let that be the last time I hear you speak of any kind of sex with another while I'm about to make love to you. It's just you, me, and Amara now, and I'm *very* possessive."

Seth rolled his eyes. As if he hadn't known that. Instead of saying anything, he pulled away and Tristan let him. For all the fae's big talk, he'd never do anything Seth didn't want to. Seth slowly made his way toward the pool, stripping off his shirt and jeans as he did. He hadn't worn shoes or underwear so the actions left him completely naked. He bent over to check the temperature of the pool since these were private ones that could be warmed if necessary even if they connected with the rest of the ocean in a series of tunnels. As he bent, Tristan let out a groan.

Good.

Before Seth could straighten, Tristan cupped Seth's ass and squeezed. Seth gripped the edge of the pool and let out a shaky breath.

"Goddess, you're fucking sexy," Tristan said softly then moved away.

Seth would have complained at the lack of touch, but as he turned, he came face to face with Tristan's very erect cock.

Speechless, he leaned forward and licked the tip. Tristan grunted and pulled back.

"You promised me an underwater blowjob," Tristan said, his voice a growl. "And if you suck me off right here, I'll blow before I can experience it. And I *want* to experience it all with you. And when we're done, I'll let you fuck me, Seth. Or do you want me to fuck you? Just say the word and it's yours."

Seth swallowed and slowly slid into the pool, his eyes on Tristan. "I want you to fuck me first." He grinned then. "You think you can get it up right after I make you come, old man?"

Tristan lifted his lip in a snarl and pushed Seth back. Seth laughed as he slid down into the pool. He kept his human form since they were going to have sex but he could still see, hear, and talk under water like he could in mer form, just as he could breathe easily. With the tail, he was stronger and faster, and it added an extra layer of protection, but he didn't need that when all he wanted was the man in front of him.

Tristan wouldn't be able to hear Seth when he was underwater, but that was okay. Seth would be able to find out exactly what the man liked as soon as he had his lips on him. He swam closer and put his hands on Tristan's thighs. The other man slid his hand into the water and down to Seth's shoulder. With the other hand, he tangled his fingers in Seth's hair. Seth smiled before licking up the long length of his lover. He could hear the groan from above the water and went to work.

He sucked on the tip, letting his magic seep out of him to create a steady vibration in the water. It would warm up the molecules and send a tremor down Tristan's dick. The man would feel as if he had a constant vibrator on him without even having to move from the pool.

"Seth!" Tristan called out and pulled on his hair.

Seth sucked the man down to the back of his throat, hummed, then let him slide out before he lifted his head from the water. "Yes, fae?"

"That thing with the water?" Tristan swallowed hard. "What the fuck?"

"I'm a merman, Tristan. I can do all sorts of things with water."

Tristan's eyes narrowed. "Damn. How the hell did I not know this? And you didn't tell me, meaning you wanted to see if I'd come with just that vibration alone. Well, dear, I almost did, and because of that, next time we're in my realm, I'll show you a few tricks I've learned in my nine hundred years." He put his hand on the back of Seth's head. "Now get back down there and suck me off."

Seth chuckled, kissed his mate, then slid back down into the water to do as he was told. It wasn't as if he would have fought that command hard anyway. He wanted his lips around Tristan's dick. He wanted to make the man come until he was spent, then work him back up so he could fuck Seth. Hard.

And when they were both sated, they'd go to their room and spoon with Amara so they were rested for the trip. Sounded like a perfect plan.

He fisted Tristan's cock and pumped him, loving the way his lover's thighs strained. Seth licked his lips then went down on the fae, sucking and licking until Tristan pumped into his mouth. When the fae's dick stiffened even more and the first spurt of come landed on his tongue, Seth sucked harder, wanting every drop. Tristan's hand tightened in Seth's hair as he came and he shouted Seth's name. When Seth couldn't take it anymore, his own dick hard as a rock, he let go of his lover and lifted his head out of the water. Before he could take another breath, Tristan had his hands and mouth on him, kissing him senseless. Their mouths clashed and their bodies trembled. Tristan's cock was already hard again, pressing against the line of Seth's hip.

"I want you, Seth." Tristan waved his hand out and lube magically appeared on the side of the pool.

Tristan snorted. "You seriously just used your powers to get lube? Where the hell was it to begin with?"

"In my pants pocket, but I didn't feel like getting out of the water." Tristan kissed him again. "Now shut up and turn around. Grip the edge of the pool and let me love you." With one last kiss, he twisted Seth around and Seth let out a groan of his own.

Seth gripped the edge like Tristan had asked, then gasped as Tristan probed him with one lubed finger.

"I've never done it in the water like this," Tristan said softly before kissing Seth's shoulder. "If it hurts because of it, let me know and we'll get out."

Seth shook his head. "I'm a merman. Water is... different for me. I want you in here, in me. Okay?"

Tristan kissed the side of his neck then nodded. "Okay, baby. Now lie forward and think of England."

Seth snorted before letting out a grunt as Tristan slid one finger in and out of him. Seth leaned back so his head rested on Tristan's shoulder.

"More," Seth whispered. "Give me more."

"So greedy," Tristan whispered. "But I'm impatient so I'll agree. We can go slow with Amara so she'll end up a teased mess."

"Deal. Now fuck me."

Seth's breath quickened, and Tristan worked another finger into him, then another. Soon he was panting with need and Tristan was doing the same. When Tristan pushed forward, the head of his cock breaching Seth's ass, they both froze.

"Okay, baby?" Tristan asked, his words low. He kissed up Seth's neck, soothing.

"I'm good," Seth gritted out. He felt so full, and yet Tristan hadn't even pushed all the way in. If it felt this good now, he couldn't even comprehend how good it would feel when he was all the way in.

"Yeah, Seth, you are," Tristan whispered. And with that, he slowly worked his way in and out of him.

Seth's fingers on the edge of the pool tightened at the sensation of Tristan pushing into him then sliding out. Slow. Real slow. He couldn't catch his breath, couldn't think of what it meant or what was to come. He could only *feel*.

"Harder," Seth grunted.

Tristan didn't say anything, but he picked up the pace. He had one hand on Tristan's hip, the other on his chest. Soon they were both writhing, panting, fucking and making love. The water around them splashed over the edge. When Tristan reached around and cupped Seth's balls before gripping his dick, Seth came.

Just one touch and he came.

He shouted Tristan's name, and Tristan did the same for him as he came, as well. Still inside him, Tristan leaned on Seth's back and caught his breath. Seth did the same, leaning forward on the edge of the pool, his body shaking. He'd lost another of his virginities, and damn if he wasn't happy he'd waited. He wasn't sure if it would have been as good with anyone else. Amara and Tristan were *his*—despite the lack of bond—and that was all that mattered.

Seth opened his mouth to speak, to try and say something about how much it all meant to him, but stiffened as he sensed another presence beneath them. He pulled away, wincing as Tristan slid out of him. Tristan must have felt the other as well because he turned, his magic rising in the room. Since it was a natural pool with a shallow section that led to tunnels and the deeper sections of the ocean, everything was connected.

"It's another merman. Four, actually. Part of a school." Seth cursed. "Get out of the water, Tristan."

"I'm not leaving you."

"And your magic is no match in our waters. Get out and protect me from above. You can see me clearly, and I won't leave your sight. I promise." With a quick kiss to Tristan's lips, Seth lowered himself fully in the water and shifted to his mer form.

"What do you want?" he called out to the four mermen. They weren't armed from what he could see, but that didn't mean they didn't have other plans. "Why are you in Calypso's pool without permission?" Caly would never have let another in her pools with things so tense with Amara's realm.

"We aren't here to harm you," the one up front said. Seth didn't recognize him, nor did he the others. "We are here with a warning."

Seth's jaw tightened. "And what warning would that be? Coming into our pool without permission is a threat, not a warning. You should know that."

"There are whispers of the siren, young one. If you do not end her now, the sirens will come for her and spark war. Is a woman who is not your mate worth the death of so many of your brethren?"

Seth's eyes narrowed. What. The. Fuck. "Get your condescending asses and your warnings out of this pool, or I will show you the power that lies within my veins. And that fae up there? He has more power in his pinky than the four of you together." It was a guess, but he was pretty sure he was right. With Tristan out of the water but in line of sight, he was far more powerful than swimming alongside him with the Kiss of Life.

"Take care of her," the man said once more then lifted his chin. "Or we will."

Seth growled and darted toward them. The others tried to move away, but Seth was far faster than he looked. His tail flashed out and knocked into two of them, breaking one's arm and the other's nose. His fist landed on another's cheek and he twisted to slap his fin on the fourth's side, most likely bruising the merman's ribs. He'd done it in a flash, and soon, the small school swam away, stunned and hurting.

When he was sure they were gone, he shot up out of the pool and landed on his feet, shifting in mid air.

Tristan came up to him, his eyes wide, but he didn't say anything.

"We have a problem," Seth said, his voice full of anger.

"I figured," Tristan said softly. "I think we should wake Amara and go. We don't have much time."

"No. We don't. And it's going to be harder than we thought." And with that sentiment, he turned on his heel and walked naked to their room. He needed to get his mates out of there before another school approached. They needed to get to the siren realm and meet the queen. He didn't know what they would do afterward, but if they didn't do this, others would get hurt. They had to face this head-on, and he prayed that Amara would find the strength within her to stay by their sides. Because he knew she was strong enough. Only he didn't think she did.

And that was dangerous. Could prove deadly.

CHAPTER 7

Tristan did his best to not let his powers lash out, but it was damned hard when all he wanted to do was wrap his mates up in cotton wool and hide them from danger. Of course, that wouldn't be happening anytime soon, and frankly, wouldn't help much anyway.

"What do you mean you were attacked?" Amara gasped. She slid her hands down Seth's now clothed body as if checking for injuries, then did the same to Tristan. "Why didn't you tell me *before* we left Caly's place? Instead, you just woke me up and tucked me to your side without more than a few words, saying we needed to hurry. You need to tell me things." She looked at both of them. "I thought we already had the discussion of how I need to be kept in the loop. I might be the only girl in this relationship and the one who is newest to her powers, but I deserve to know everything."

Tristan let out a breath. They were in the forest on the edge of the wolf den—Hunter's den, actually—within the human realm. There wasn't an easy way into the siren realm from the mer realm. If Amara had been born a siren, it would have been different, but as she hadn't, they'd had to go through the only portal he knew of. And that was within the human realm. The humans, as they were diluted descendants of the paranormals, held all the portals to all the realms. They just didn't know it. And most portals were such that one couldn't just magically show up at the edge. The three of them needed to hike a bit to where he knew the portal had last been. He just hoped it hadn't moved in the past century, or he'd have to call up Dante and the others and see if they knew where it was. He didn't want to worry everyone more than they probably already were. Amara had called the girls to tell them what she was, but that was it. He was sure the old dragon and the others probably knew of the whispers and rumors, but they hadn't contacted them about it. He knew if it came down to it, the others would come to their sides, but he didn't want to risk them. Not yet.

"You deserve to know everything," Tristan finally said. "But we needed to get out of there and to a place where we could talk." He looked around at the trees around them. With Hunter's den so close, they were relatively safe. This was as good a place to talk as any.

Amara folded her arms over her chest and narrowed her eyes. They'd taught her to hold her glamour so she looked like her human self, rather than the siren she was. Tristan also had a glamour on her, in case hers fell. She was still so new to all of this, and she'd readily agreed to his help.

"Don't hold back, okay?" she said softly. "I know you guys want to protect me, and I get it, but I can't protect myself if I don't know everything." Something passed over her eyes, and Tristan took a step toward her.

"What is it? What just went through your mind?" He reached out and cupped her chin. Seth stood on her other side, his hand on her hip.

"It's nothing."

He shook his head and pinched her chin so she was forced to look into his eyes. Her mouth parted and her eyes dilated. Interesting. He filed that information away for later and kept his mind on the task at hand.

"You can't tell me it's nothing after your little speech right there, little siren. We're safe where we are for a bit." He held up his hands, his powers reaching out to surround them in a protective ward. "What are you hiding, darling?"

She pressed her lips together. "Fine. The girls know, but that's it. I don't want to make a big deal about it, but if I don't get it off my chest, you'll just try to figure it out anyway." She pulled away and wrapped her arms around her stomach. When he and Seth both moved to get closer, she shook her head. It burned, but he let it happen. If she needed to hold herself apart to get through what she needed to say, he'd let it happen. For now.

"Every time you talk about strength or protecting me, it just reminds me I didn't have that before. I've never had it. My girls are my family. Why? Because the family I was born to meant nothing. *I* meant nothing. My mom killed herself when I was a little girl. Probably because she couldn't take it anymore."

Seth let out a breath beside him and moved closer. Amara held up her hand but their mate ignored it.

"I need to hold you. You're going to have to deal with it."

Tristan liked the firmness in Seth's tone but didn't move forward. He wouldn't crowd her right then.

Amara let out a shaky breath. "My mom killed herself so Dad wouldn't. He used to beat her, break her, use her. And when she died, he turned his...attentions on me."

Tristan let out a growl and the wards around them pulsed a dangerous red.

Amara's eyes widened as she looked around them, and then she met Tristan's gaze even as she leaned into Seth. "He never touched me in that way. That came out wrong. I'm sorry."

"You have nothing to be sorry for," he bit out.

Seth gave him a warning look, and he tried to control himself.

"My dad beat me when he could and broke my bones. I was never strong enough to protect myself, and I couldn't leave until I finished school. The authorities did nothing because he hid it well." She swallowed hard. "And because I lied to them. He told me he'd kill me if I told anyone, and I believed him. I was young and stupid and broken. So I let him hit me. But when I grew up, I ran away. I didn't have a home, I didn't have a family. But then I met Lily and the others and they became the only family I had. I'm only telling you this because well, you're both mine, and you deserve to know. And I'm telling you now because I need you both to know that I'm finding my strength. You don't have to protect me."

Tristan stepped toward her and cupped her face. His jaw ached and he unclenched his teeth. "You are strong, Amara. I don't know why you don't think you are. To survive what you did and be able to...be with us as you are, that is strength." He'd almost said love, but as they hadn't professed those feelings yet, he waited. "We will always protect you, Amara. But that's not because we think you can't do it yourself, it's because it's our vow, our duty, our hope that we do so. When you grow in your powers, you will do the same for us. It's how matings work. We protect each other. I might be older than both of you by centuries, but I'm not so old as to think a woman can't take care of herself. You are a warrior in your own right, and you will be a warrior in every way possible when the time comes."

"As for your family," Seth added, "the girls are your family. *We* are your family. And with us, you have more than one home. When we get through the siren...mess, then we'll see how those homes work, but we're it, Amara. You have us, no matter what."

She licked her lips, tears filling her eyes. "You're both my home. I know that now."

Tristan shuddered then kissed her softly. "I love you," he whispered. He stiffened, as he hadn't meant for that to slip out, but now that it had, he was happy about it. "I love you, Amara. I wanted you from the moment I first saw you, but I loved you the moment you took a chance on the unknown."

He turned to Seth. "And it's the same for you. I love you, my Seth."

Seth cupped the back of Tristan's head. "I love you both." He kissed him, then Amara.

Amara looked between them, her eyes wide, but a small smile on her face. "I love you both, as well. And I can't believe I'm saying that as we're hiding in a forest on the way to the siren realm. Nothing is how I thought it would be, but I'm happy." She took a deep breath. "Now let's get through to the realm and see what we must do. I don't want to wait anymore for the bond. I don't want to wait to see what the queen will do. I feel as though if we wait for her to come to us, it won't end as well."

Tristan nodded. "I agree." He ran a hand over his chin. "The portal is close. I can feel it." He met the others' gazes and frowned. "I hope you two can feel it as well once we're closer."

"Well, you *are* older," Seth said with a smirk.

Tristan punched his lover in the shoulder, and the merman just stood there. Damn.

Amara put her hands on her hips. "And when we get there? What are we going to do exactly?"

Tristan answered, "If I remember correctly, there is a roadside inn right when you go through the portal. It's been a century since I've done so, but in non-human realms, things tend to move slower than the human one. We'll still be a ways from queen's domain, or rather where she gathers her people. That will give us time to regroup and make sure we're...presentable for the queen."

Amara shuddered but nodded. "Sounds like a plan."

He gripped her hand and let the wards fall around them. They wouldn't be able to pass through the portal with the ward bubble around them, sadly. Tristan put Amara behind him and Seth took the rear. Amara might be able to fight a little, but she didn't have the experience they had yet. He would just have to teach her. Because he'd be damned if he'd force her to waste away behind a locked door even if he had wanted to wrap her in cotton wool before.

They walked another half mile or so and Tristan sighed as the tingling sensation of a portal crawled over his skin.

"Wow," Amara said from behind him. "That's...different."

"It's your first real portal," Seth said from behind them. "Or at least one we didn't make since your change."

"Let's get through it before I change my mind and say we go hide in a cave somewhere until the queen forgets about me."

Tristan turned around and frowned. "We can do that. We can hide." It would go against all he believed in, but to keep his mates safe, he would.

Amara shook her head then lifted onto her toes and kissed his chin. "I'll fight. I don't know if I can do exactly what needs to be done, but maybe words will be enough." She didn't look like she believed it, but Tristan nodded then met Seth's gaze. Yes, both of them understood. Amara wouldn't have to kill the queen if that's what it came down to. Tristan and Seth would. They were warriors, and Amara was not. Yet. There was no reason she should have to do something that hurt her when they could do it for her. As for a war between realms, that could possibly be avoided. If the queen were really out of favor like the others thought, and Tristan figured that had to be the case from what he knew, then his people as well as Seth's should be safe.

He turned away from them once more and held out his arms. The portal shimmered once before fading away again.

"Well, hell." He cursed again and closed his eyes, only to stop when Amara put her hand on his arm.

"I think it needs to be me." She frowned as he looked down at her. "I don't know how I know that, but I think I need to be the one that opens it. You need to preserve your energy, and Seth is still tired from fighting the school."

"I'm not that tired," Seth grumbled but sighed. "But I think Amara is right. She's a siren and she's going home, for lack of a better word, for the first time. It needs to be her."

"And if the queen notices?"

"She's going to notice my presence one way or another, we might as well get *into* the realm before we freak out." With that, she held out her hands and scrunched her face. She had no idea what she was doing, but at least she was trying. Tristan couldn't be prouder.

When she opened her mouth and began to sing, Tristan took two staggered steps backwards.

Her voice. The beauty. Holy shit.

"Amara," he whispered in awe. Seth came to his side and put his hand on his shoulder.

"Holy fuck," his mate said softly. "Now I know why men eagerly went to their deaths. Her song, Tristan. Her *song*."

Her hair fanned around her, and though he couldn't see her face, he knew he'd see the ink on her body, on her soul. She was a true siren, her song that of purpose and eternity. When the portal shimmered back into existence, she held out one arm and made a motion with her hand to bring them forward. He and Seth stepped toward her, gripped her hands, and took another step with her. Between one breath and the next, they found themselves within the siren realm, the portal shutting tightly behind them. Amara had stopped singing, her breath coming in pants.

"That was…unexpected," she said softly.

He met Seth's gaze and knew the other man's thoughts were on the same path as his. If that was her power when she had no training, it was no wonder the queen wanted Amara's line gone. Amara's song spoke of a magic and ability that was immense in both greatness and strength. He'd wanted to fall to his knees and let her take him wherever she wished. It was only because he knew who she was beneath that power and how scared she would be to find out the depth of it alone, that he'd stayed on his feet. They would have to get her trained as quickly as possible. His friend Malik might be able to help with that as he trained many paranormals, no matter what realm they came from. But first, they had to deal with the queen.

Thankfully, the inn that he'd seen before still stood, and not much else had changed in this part of the realm. It looked like any part of the human realm, with its large fields and far off forests. However, the purple sky with swirls of moving stars was the only thing that spoke of the differentness.

"The queen's castle is behind that tree line," Tristan said. "We should be able to get a room in the inn tonight and head there in the morning. It will give us time to reenergize."

"Let's get it done, then," Amara said, her voice still breathy. "I can't believe I just sang. I didn't know I *could* sing like that."

"It's inherent in you, and you will learn to control it," Seth added. "But damn, honey, you were magnificent."

Tristan agreed and took their hands. "Let's get inside before we're seen." They went inside and met the innkeeper, a small older siren that looked at him curiously but kept her mouth shut. They got a room on the second floor—one where it would still be easy to jump out of the window if needed—and paid.

Seth sighed and rubbed the back of his neck as they walked into the room and locked the door behind them.

"I'm going to go soak in the tub for a bit and reclaim the rest of my energy. I know it's not the ocean, but it's fine." He shrugged, and Tristan walked over to him and kissed him deeply.

"We'll be out here when you're done."

Seth winked, and Tristan relaxed. It seemed his mate wanted to make sure Amara and Tristan had time alone together. Goddess he loved that man.

Seth closed the bathroom door behind him, and Tristan slid the pack off his shoulders so he could face Amara. "You were beautiful out there. Powerful. I want you to understand that. Even with no training, you were *power*. I was in awe of you, Amara. I *am* in awe of you."

She smiled at him then. "I kind of kicked ass, didn't I?"

He licked his lips and leaned forward. "Yeah, you did, and you'll only get stronger as you learn to use your gifts. I'm proud of you, Amara. I hope you know that."

She lifted up on her toes and kissed his lips since he had leaned down so she could reach. "Being with you makes me stronger. Same as with Seth. We're great on our own, but we aren't whole. I know fate made the choice for us, but I'd have taken you and Seth as my own even without that." She paused. "I wanted the both of you, I *love* the both of you, even if I don't feel the tug, don't feel the bond. That means something to me, Tristan."

He cupped her face. "It means something to me, as

well. Now let me make love to you, little siren. Let me feel you beneath me as I fill you up."

"I thought you'd never ask."

They stripped one another slowly, taking their time to enjoy the touches, the feel of one another. Soon he was above her, his cock sliding between her folds as he teased her. She arched up into him and he took her nipple into his mouth. Her breasts were glorious, overfilling his hands and making him want to fuck them. Later, he promised himself. There would be time for that and more later.

When their eyes met, he slid deep inside her, their breaths syncing as he slowly pumped in and out of her. She wrapped her legs around him and pulled him deeper.

"Fuck the bond," he growled as he fucked her. "Fuck it. I have you. I have him. I don't need the bond, Amara. I just need both of you. You're more important than that." With each sentence, he thrust into her, harder and harder until they both cascaded over the edge.

She cupped his face as she came, her mouth parted. When she took a deep breath, her pussy clenched around him. "I want the bond. I want to show you what I feel. But if what happens next with the queen doesn't allow the bond to happen, I won't leave. I am yours as you are mine. Forever, Tristan. Okay? Forever."

He crushed his mouth to hers and pumped into her again, his cock already hard once more. His heart broke at the lack of bond, but he knew he'd heal. He'd do anything for Seth and Amara, even break himself and his future to ensure the two of them could bond. They were more important than he was. If he could find a way to keep them as one, he would. If he could make it so the *three* of them were one, even better.

No matter what, these two were his. But he'd be damned if he'd allow a curse that occurred before Amara's birth to take the rest of what should be his.

They would fix it. He vowed it, his powers sliding over his skin as he made love to his mate. The bond would come, but if it didn't, then fuck it. Amara and Seth were his.

And that was all that mattered.

CHAPTER 8

Amara stood at the edge of the castle grounds and tried not to let the rapid beat of her heart scare the shit out of her. This felt like a dream, yet she knew it wasn't. Everything she'd thought she knew before this day had crashed around her, and now here she stood, in front of the siren queen's castle, standing between her two men and praying she wouldn't lose either of them in the fallout.

She let out a breath, rolled her shoulders, and then reached out for both men's hands. "Let's do this."

Tristan looked down at her, his face solemn. "We won't let her hurt you."

Seth nudged her. "Hopefully, she'll just break the curse and we can go home and have cake. How does that sound?"

She smiled despite herself. These two were so different, yet so adorably hers. But in order to make that permanent in truth, she needed to deal with one thing first.

The queen.

"Cake sounds perfect," she said after a moment. "Let's just hope for cake."

They each squeezed her hand, and she froze as the large doors in front of her opened without them knocking. Well, that made sense, as they had been just standing there for a bit trying to prepare themselves. There was no way they had gone unseen since then. She was just happy that she'd had the little time she had.

Tristan went first, and she followed with Seth close behind her. They might be one unit, but Tristan had far more experience in courts and the like. The large stone building had ivy running along the outside and vines with roses and other deep red flowers on the inside. The beauty of it would have awed her, if she hadn't known the person in charge had killed Amara's entire line before she'd even been born.

If Amara hadn't been struck by lightning, the queen never would have noticed her. But if she hadn't been changed, hadn't been altered in some fundamental way, she never would have met Tristan and Seth. And they were worth far more than what the queen had to offer.

The queen only held death and banishment and Amara knew there would be no future there for her.

Ahead of them sat a throne that rivaled any royalty's she'd seen in movies. A tall woman with long, raven hair wrapped in an ornate ponytail that slid over her shoulder sat in the chair. Her green eyes weren't a normal color, but rather a bright shade that seemed to light from within. She had strong cheekbones and pale, pale skin. If anything, she looked like a true Evil Queen. And that only worried Amara more than she already was.

"I cannot believe you have the audacity to walk through my doors as you have," the queen crooned. Her voice was a deep, throaty purr, and it scared the hell out of Amara.

"Queen," Tristan said deeply. "We are here—"

"I know why you are here," she cut him off and stood. Her long dress draped around her, showing off her curves. "You're lucky you're a Conclave member or I'd sing you to your death, fae."

Tristan growled. "I'm far older than you, Queen. It's best you remember that."

The queen snapped her teeth then smiled at Amara. "You've come to me, young siren. You didn't glamour yourself, I'm surprised."

Amara raised her chin, knowing it showed off her marks even more. She'd decided to come as she was now, rather than who she'd been before. They were there for a future and to face their problems, hiding her ink and skin would have been counterproductive.

"Queen," she said. She didn't bow. For some reason, she knew if she did, the queen would think she'd won. "I am here to ask for you to break the curse you put on my line before I was born. I do not want your throne or any life other than the life I could have with my mates. I won't come for anything you hold dear or rise to power like you thought the others would. I am just me. Amara. I ask this of you. Please."

She hadn't rehearsed what she would say, but that seemed like the best thing. Maybe her pleading would work. Because if it didn't, she'd have to decide if running for her life with her two mates without a bond would be worth it. If she didn't do that...well, then she'd have to end the curse one way or another. And from the snarl on the queen's face, they both knew it.

"You want me to break the curse? And why do you think I'd do that? Your line *earned* that."

"How did they do that?" Seth asked. "By trying to take down a monarchy which clearly threatens the realm? Amara wasn't alive then. How do you blame her for the past?"

"I can do as I please," the queen snapped. "Your line was *eradicated*. And yet the Conclave chose to give you powers? You're an abomination."

The lightning hadn't exactly worked like that, but

Amara wasn't about to correct her. It seemed as though she were on the edge as it was.

"There are other ways to break the curse," Amara said softy, her voice calmer than she expected. Both Seth and Tristan stiffened, though they'd done it so subtlety she wasn't sure anyone would have noticed. She just happened to know their bodies well.

The queen tilted her head. "You're threatening me, young one? You don't even have full control of your powers, and yet you come to me with your threats."

"We're here because it's protocol," Tristan bit out. "A new member of the realm needs to present his or herself to the powers that be. We're here, and now you've seen her."

"And yet you want me to remove a curse." The queen shook her head. "No, I don't think I will do that. In fact, I do believe a lesson is in order." She raised her head and opened her mouth.

Amara didn't have time to think before the queen began to sing, her voice a haunting melody that spoke of powers Amara might never understand.

Seth grunted from her side before a scream ripped from him. Amara turned to him and let out a scream of her own. The queen continued to sing, and with each note, it looked as if Seth caved in on himself.

"She's drying him out!" Tristan called out and took a step toward the queen. Amara moved to Seth and caught his head as he fell backwards. His skin began to look brittle, as if he were losing all the water in his system. As a merman, it was even more dangerous for him.

Tears slid down her cheeks and she did the only thing she could do.

She sang.

Seth gasped for air as Tristan worked his magic, trying to stop the queen. And while this happened, Amara sang a song of healing. Again, it was innate to her, as if the songs had been etched on her bones, in her soul. She would have to think later about why she knew these songs without ever hearing them before, but for now, she would take what she could and try to heal one of the pieces of her heart.

The magic slid over her skin like a warm blanket as she let her voice do the work. Seth gripped her hand and met her eyes. Tears slid down her cheeks, but all she could feel was Seth's pain. She lowered her voice, letting the song take root as Seth began to fill out again, his breathing calming.

The queen cursed and took a staggered step back as Amara raised her chin. Tristan had his arms up, fae magic swirling around him. He looked like a god, a fae prince with a power that should bring fear and awe; instead, it only made her love him more.

"You should never have been brought to us," the queen

spat. "I will *never* break the curse. Your whole line should have learned its place long ago."

Others began to crowd around them, but the look of menace and fear on their faces wasn't directed toward Amara...but at the queen. It seemed what the others had said was correct, the queen wasn't in favor.

"I will kill you, Amara. I will take your breath, twist your soul. And when I'm through with you, I will do the same to Seth and Tristan. They should never have brought you here. It just made it easier for me."

She held out her arms, but Amara didn't flinch. She knew what she had to do. She'd known it from the beginning. The queen would never relent. Even if they survived what was to come and hid, they would always be on the run. The rest of her family, Lily, Jamie, and the rest, would always be in danger because of her. The others had all faced their fears when it came to those that had wanted to hurt them, and now it was Amara's turn.

Amara stood, her own arms out. "I'm sorry," she said to her men. Tristan moved toward her as Seth stood up on shaky legs. "I'm so sorry."

And with that, she sang.

It wasn't a song of healing nor one to open a portal. Those had a beauty that called to her soul. This one had a dark beauty of its own, but it wasn't her soul it called to.

The queen wanted the other realms, wanted to show the world she had power. She would stop at nothing to take what she wanted, and Amara couldn't allow that to happen—even if it broke a part of her to do so.

Her men held her hands, bringing her strength she hadn't known she craved as she sang the shadowed melody of darkness. The queen's eyes widened and she clutched her throat, unable to continue her own song.

It seemed the queen had been right to fear Amara's line. For Amara was far more powerful than she. Amara continued to sing, her melody reaching the queen's hardened soul. Amara changed the lyrics then, twisting when she could have soothed. It broke her to think about what she was doing, so she didn't think, she only acted. She would deal with the consequences, the mark on her soul and the fallout with Seth and Tristan when the time came.

The queen screamed and fell to her knees. Sweat dripped down Amara's spine and temples as she continued her song. When her men held her close, whispering soothing words and running their hands through her hair, she knew she could lean on them.

Soon, she closed her mouth, her song finished. The queen no more.

Her legs gave out and tears spilled down her cheeks. She'd just killed someone. Ended their life so she could live...so her family could live. Perhaps if the queen hadn't attacked Seth as she had, Amara might have found another way. But with that one act, the queen had set her fate.

"Little siren," Tristan whispered before kissing her softly. "Darling. It's okay. You can breathe. We're here."

Seth whispered much of the same, his hands on her back as he kissed her neck. "We're here."

She didn't know how long she let herself sway in their arms. Her body hurt, her soul a bit tired from what she'd done. She didn't know the ramifications, the effect on her own future after what she'd done, but hopefully, no matter what happened, her men were safe. They were all that mattered.

She opened her mouth to speak, but froze as something so sweet, so hot, so *everything* snapped into place.

"The bond," Seth gasped.

Amara smiled despite what had happened moments before and threw her arms around her men's shoulders. "The bond."

Tristan smiled as well before kissing her. "I feel you, darling. I feel both of you. You're mine now. Now and forever."

"I never knew it would feel like this," Seth said in awe.

She could feel their souls tangle with hers, as if the world had stopped and it was only the three of them. While she would have stayed there, letting the bond settle as she got to know her men all over again, someone cleared their throat from beside them. Then the reality of where they were and what had happened with the queen settled into her.

She turned toward a group of thirty people or so and swallowed hard as they each knelt in front of her.

"My queen," one of the men in front said. "I am David, a siren of a different line. We...we wanted to say thank you for freeing us. The former queen held our lines hostage for far too long, and none of us were powerful enough to stop it."

Her men stood on either side of her, though they didn't hold her hands. It was enough that she could feel them at her sides and in her heart.

That was something she would have to get used to, but hell, she loved it. She loved them.

Wait. "Did you just call me your queen?" She shook her head. "I'm no queen. I'm just me."

"There's nothing *just* about you," Tristan said softly before addressing the others. "Because she killed the former queen, are you saying she is the new monarch?"

David nodded. "That's how it's always worked." He frowned. "I know you're new and have no idea about our realm, but we *need* a king or queen. It's not just for decisions, but how our songs work. There needs to be order, and frankly, we have been in chaos for too long with the former queen."

Amara shook her head and licked her lips. Seth put his hand on her back and she settled ever so slightly. "I have no idea what I'm doing, and I've been in the siren realm for all of a day. I'm not fit to be queen."

"That makes you the perfect queen," David insisted. "We don't need someone to rule with an iron fist. We need a voice, a song of reason." He held up his hands when she opened her mouth to counter. "I'm not saying you should jump on the throne right now, but when you feel ready to come back to the realm, we will be here. And when you *do* come back, if you still feel you cannot be here as a presence of hope for small amounts of time, then we will see how we can move the crown to another. We aren't a fighting people, Amara. We just need some form of order for our songs to be melodic."

It was all too much for her, but she knew if she said no right then, she might hurt the others in the room that had such hopeful expressions on their faces.

"I...I need time to think."

"Of course," David said and nodded at the others around them. As one, the sirens stood up and smiled at her.

It was all so surreal. She was a siren, a mated siren. And now, a freaking queen? Not to mention the fact that the dead body of the former queen lay a few feet away and no one had done anything about it. No love lost there, apparently. Maybe one day she would wake up from the dream, but if that meant she would lose Tristan and Seth, then maybe she wanted to stay asleep.

"We'll figure it out," Seth said softly. "We have time."

"We have all the time in the world," Tristan added, and that calmed her.

Yes, they had all the time in the world to figure out the next step. That was how she'd made it this far; how she'd become a siren in a world where she'd always thought she was alone. She might not know what to do next or what her life meant in the siren world, but she had her family, had her soul.

She'd found her home, and now she could be whoever she wanted to be.

She was Amara. Siren. Mate. Queen. And home.

ELIANA

The pink line mocked her. It screamed at her even though it was just a damned pink line on a home pregnancy test. It had never occurred to Eliana that she would be the last mateless lightning-struck of the seven. It also had never occurred to her that she'd have her heart broken by someone she'd thought would make being with a human, and being mortal, okay.

Not to mention, she'd never thought she would end up pregnant and alone.

But the seven positive pregnancy tests that littered the floor next to the bottles of water so she could actually take said tests didn't lie.

Malik had dumped her like she was yesterday's trash, and she should have been over it already. She'd gotten over the men in the past that had broken up with her for one reason or another easily, yet this seemed different.

Yeah, he hadn't been her true half or whatever since he'd been human and all, but hell, she'd thought he was the one.

And now she was pregnant with his baby and he wasn't answering his phone.

Eliana, the last lightning-struck female and human in her own right, was royally screwed.

And the others didn't even know the half of it yet.

Well, shit.

EPILOGUE

Amara lifted her head and leaned against Seth as he slid into her from behind. Tristan groaned beneath her, his hands on her hips. Both of her men worked as one, her fae fucking her cunt while her merman fucked her ass, their bodies sweat-slick. She'd woken up in Tristan's bed with both men sucking her breasts and readying her for their attention.

It seriously was the best way to wake up.

Seth slid out of her and she moaned. Then she found herself on her back as Tristan pounded her into the bed. Her fae prince groaned and she laughed. She couldn't help it. She loved it when their Seth surprised the both of them.

Seth held onto Tristan's hips and slowly worked his way into their mate. The bond flared between them all and love poured into her soul. Tears slid down her cheeks as they made love this way and every way. They were hers in truth, in body and soul, and she knew this was her fate, her future.

Tristan made sweet love to her as Seth did the same to him. She put her hands on both of them, needing them close as she came on a wave. Her men followed her, their voices growls as they shouted their passion, their love.

When they were finally able to breathe, she found herself spooned between both of them as Tristan used a warm, damp cloth on her. She pillowed her head on Seth's arm and smiled at him.

"I would say we need to wake up that way every morning, but I might not make it," she teased.

Seth winked and kissed her softly. "We'll just have to find inventive ways to wake you up, then."

She groaned. "I might run out of energy."

"Don't worry, little siren," Tristan said smoothly from behind her. "We'll find ways. We always do."

Her phone buzzed then, the alarm going off. "We're going to be late," she said as she sank into their holds. "I promised the girls I would be at Dante's Circle to see what Eliana needs to talk about, and I don't want to be the last one there."

Tristan gripped her hip and kissed her shoulder. Seth's fingers played with her nipples and she moaned before sitting up.

"Hey, I wasn't done with those," Seth said with a smile.

She batted him off and did the same to Tristan. "Stop it, both of you. I need to shower. Alone." She narrowed her eyes when both men leaned back, their cocks hard and standing at attention. "We have like seven showers in this home. Use them. Separately. I don't want to be late. I haven't seen the others since my change, and it was only because I promised to be there *on time* that they didn't all show up on our doorstep last night."

"You're beautiful when you're on a mission," Tristan said with a grin.

"You're beautiful always," Seth added.

Amara stood at the edge of the bed, her hands on her hips. "I love you both, but get clean you dirty, dirty men of mine. I will not be late. They will all know the reason why."

Tristan shrugged. "Almost all of them are newly mated. They'll understand."

"That's true enough," Seth said.

She rolled her eyes. She never once thought she'd have the kind of life she had now. She was the queen of the sirens, the voice with a song of truth and power. And yet she didn't live in the siren realm, not fully, not yet. She had her men, her powers, and her future.

There were hundreds of details to see to, and thousands more unknown, but she wasn't alone in her decisions and that made it all worth it. No matter what happened next with her friends or with any of the realms that her new family was part of, she knew she could handle it.

Because Amara wasn't alone anymore. She had a family. A home. She had everything she needed. And all it had taken was a leap of faith and a song sung in hope and destiny.

For an immortal with a lifetime of lifetimes ahead of her, that sounded like a perfect plan to her.

THE END

Next up in Dante's Circle series comes the dramatic conclusion of the lightning-struck. Eliana and Malik find their own in Prowled Darkness.

A NOTE FROM CARRIE ANN

Thank you so much for reading An Immortal's Song! I do hope if you liked this story, that you would please leave a review! Reviews help authors and readers.

Thank you so much for going on this journey with me and I do hope you enjoyed my Dante's Circle series. Without you readers, I wouldn't be where I am today.

If you want to make sure you know what's coming next from me, you can sign up for my newsletter at www. CarrieAnnRyan.com; follow me on twitter at @Carrie-AnnRyan, or like my Facebook page. I also have a Face-book Fan Club where we have trivia, chats, and other goodies. You guys are the reason I get to do what I do and I thank you.

Make sure you're signed up for my MAILING LIST

so you can know when the next releases are available as well as find giveaways and FREE READS.

Happy Reading!

Carrie Ann

Dante's Circle Series:

Book 1: Dust of My Wings

Book 2: Her Warriors' Three Wishes

Book 3: An Unlucky Moon

The Dante's Circle Box Set (Contains Books 1-3)

Book 3.5: His Choice

Book 4: Tangled Innocence

Book 5: Fierce Enchantment

Book 6: An Immortal's Song

Book 7: Prowled Darkness

Book 8: Dante's Circle Reborn

The Complete Dante's Circle Series (Contains Books 1-7)

ABOUT THE AUTHOR

Carrie Ann Ryan is the New York Times and USA Today bestselling author of contemporary and paranormal romance. Her works include the Montgomery Ink, Redwood Pack, Talon Pack, and Gallagher Brothers series, which have sold over 2.0 million books worldwide. She started writing while in graduate school for her advanced degree in chemistry and hasn't stopped since. Carrie Ann has written over fifty novels and novellas with more in the works. When she's not writing about bearded tattooed men or alpha wolves that need to find their mates, she's reading as much as she can and exploring the world of baking and gourmet cooking.

www.CarrieAnnRyan.com

MORE FROM CARRIE ANN RYAN

Montgomery Ink:

Book 0.5: Ink Inspired
Book 0.6: Ink Reunited
Book 1: Delicate Ink
Book 1.5: Forever Ink
Book 2: Tempting Boundaries
Book 3: Harder than Words
Book 4: Written in Ink
Book 4.5: Hidden Ink
Book 5: Ink Enduring
Book 6: Ink Exposed
Book 6.5: Adoring Ink
Book 6.6: Love, Honor, & Ink
Book 7: Inked Expressions
Book 7.3: Dropout

Book 7.5: Executive Ink
Book 8: Inked Memories
Book 8.5: Inked Nights
Book 8.7: Second Chance Ink

Montgomery Ink: Colorado Springs
Book 1: Fallen Ink
Book 2: Restless Ink
Book 3: Jagged Ink

The Gallagher Brothers Series:
A Montgomery Ink Spin Off Series
Book 1: Love Restored
Book 2: Passion Restored
Book 3: Hope Restored

The Whiskey and Lies Series:
A Montgomery Ink Spin Off Series
Book 1: Whiskey Secrets
Book 2: Whiskey Reveals
Book 3: Whiskey Undone

The Fractured Connections Series:
A Montgomery Ink Spin Off Series
Book 1: Breaking Without You

The Talon Pack:

Book 1: Tattered Loyalties
Book 2: An Alpha's Choice
Book 3: Mated in Mist
Book 4: Wolf Betrayed
Book 5: Fractured Silence
Book 6: Destiny Disgraced
Book 7: Eternal Mourning
Book 8: Strength Enduring
Book 9: Forever Broken

Redwood Pack Series:
Book 1: An Alpha's Path
Book 2: A Taste for a Mate
Book 3: Trinity Bound
Redwood Pack Box Set (Contains Books 1-3)
Book 3.5: A Night Away
Book 4: Enforcer's Redemption
Book 4.5: Blurred Expectations
Book 4.7: Forgiveness
Book 5: Shattered Emotions
Book 6: Hidden Destiny
Book 6.5: A Beta's Haven
Book 7: Fighting Fate
Book 7.5: Loving the Omega
Book 7.7: The Hunted Heart
Book 8: Wicked Wolf
The Complete Redwood Pack Box Set (Contains

Books 1-7.7)

The Branded Pack Series:
(Written with Alexandra Ivy)
Book 1: Stolen and Forgiven
Book 2: Abandoned and Unseen
Book 3: Buried and Shadowed

Dante's Circle Series:
Book 1: Dust of My Wings
Book 2: Her Warriors' Three Wishes
Book 3: An Unlucky Moon
The Dante's Circle Box Set (Contains Books 1-3)
Book 3.5: His Choice
Book 4: Tangled Innocence
Book 5: Fierce Enchantment
Book 6: An Immortal's Song
Book 7: Prowled Darkness
Book 8: Dante's Circle Reborn
The Complete Dante's Circle Series (Contains Books 1-7)

Holiday, Montana Series:
Book 1: Charmed Spirits
Book 2: Santa's Executive
Book 3: Finding Abigail
The Holiday, Montana Box Set (Contains Books 1-3)

Book 4: Her Lucky Love
Book 5: Dreams of Ivory
The Complete Holiday, Montana Box Set (Contains Books 1-5)

The Happy Ever After Series:
Flame and Ink
Ink Ever After

Single Title:
Finally Found You